PARTIAL STRANGER

Equestrian Fiction by Barbara Morgenroth

Bittersweet Farm 1: Mounted
Bittersweet Farm 2: Joyful Spirit
Bittersweet Farm 3: Wingspread
Bittersweet Farm 4: Counterpoint
Bittersweet Farm 5: Calling All Comets
Bittersweet Farm 6: Kyff
Bittersweet Farm 7: Lyric Line
Bittersweet Farm 8: Tea Biscuit
Bittersweet Farm 9: Roll the Dice
Bittersweet Farm 10: Whiskey Tango
Bittersweet Farm 11: Partial Stranger

If Wishes Were Horses ~ a novella

Middle-grade

Dream Horse
Summer Horse

~BITTERSWEET FARM 11~

PARTIAL STRANGER

Barbara Morgenroth

DashingBooks

ISBN: 978-0692486184

Cover photo by Lucas Pitcher
Published by DashingBooks
Text set in Adobe Garamond

JUNE

1

"WHAT'S WRONG?" I asked, seeing Cap's face as she came onto the aisle to start the morning chores.

"Mill broke up with me." She went to get the hay cart.

"Wait!" I hurried to catch up with her. "What happened?"

Cap had spent the weekend with Mill in Virginia. Now, three days later, after being together for almost four years, the relationship had imploded. It didn't make sense.

"He found someone else?" Greer asked on her way through to her office.

I gave my sister a warning look.

"I don't know," Cap replied.

"Do you want to talk about it?" I asked.

"Cry?" Greer asked. "Or go back and beat him up?"

Taking Cap by the arm, I led her out the rear door and sat her down on a bench we had there. I said nothing as we looked out at the pasture and could see Kyff and Henry grazing.

"I thought we were going to be together for the rest of our lives," Cap said.

I didn't have any words.

"My father is a real nitwit."

"That's true."

"All I wanted was a family and the Crockers became that for me. So not only have I lost Mill, I've lost my family."

I could understand how devastated she felt. Nothing would be the same from this point forward. "Don't think I'm trying to be nosy and this conversation will be between us, but I just want to help you in whatever way I can. If I knew what he said, maybe I could begin to understand a little bit better."

"There's no reason to keep it a secret. He won't be visiting me anymore, and I won't be visiting him. That will be a dead giveaway."

"No, that's not something you'll be able to hide," I agreed.

"I arrived. Mill is straightforward. You could say blunt. He told me at the airport. I stayed there and flew to California to spend the weekend with my mother."

"Maybe if he's so straightforward he could have saved you the trip and told you on the phone."

"No, it was better if we saw each other. I'm glad I saw his face when he said this."

"What words did Mill use?"

I was seeking a clue, anything that would give me a hint what was going on for him. We had just seen him in early spring and there was no indication that they weren't very much in love.

"Teche is giving him more responsibilities and it's an unbelievable opportunity to work at that level in the world of polo. Mill doesn't know how much he'll be in America, or when his life will settle down so that there's time for me. In his mind, it's better that we should be free agents. Cut the ties. Be...single. We're young. Blah blah."

Time for her?

Just hearing these words was making me slightly queasy.

"You've had a few days to think about it. Has he said or done anything in the past month that could have been a warning for you?"

"No."

"Do you think he met someone?"

"Mill's very honest. If he did, he would have said so."

I put my arm around her. "You can think of us as your family, too. We love you. You live here, you eat all of your meals with us, you do everything with us. Gee, you're probably sick of us."

Cap managed a small smile. "Thank you. I don't know how I feel right now. These big changes in your life take time to process."

"You've had more than your share," I replied.

"You have. I didn't lose my father. He's still around being an embarrassment."

"We'll help you get through it. It's going to be a busy month.

Cap nodded, stood, and went back to the hay cart.

This is how it happened.

Life was going along smoothly, and then in a moment everything changed. It happened to me with my mother. It happened to Lockie at the Three Day. You do everything you can to right the ship of your life again, but it always lists a little.

I went back inside to do the morning chores.

***

"Inside leg, outside rein. Talia."

From the sitting trot, I pulled Kyff to a halt and turned to Lockie.

"What's going on?"

Dropping the reins, I tried to put words to emotions that had been swelling all morning.

"Get off then."

I slid to the ground and he came over to us.

"Is it possible for us to talk for a minute?"

"We're working now."

"I know but I would like to talk now."

Lockie used the roll top for a mounting block and got on Kyff, then held out his hand for my helmet. We were close enough in size that sharing was possible although not entirely comfortable.

"Why?"

"It's a relationship thing," I replied. "This is how you share your life."

He thought for a moment. "That's a good argument. What do you want to say?"

"Am I being timed?"

Lockie glanced at his eventing watch. "Go."

"Mill broke up with Cap."

"Very sad. What does that have to do with training horses this morning?"

"Wrong question. What does it have to do with us?"

"Nothing."

"She thought they were going to be together for the rest of their lives."

"I thought I was going to be a CCI Four Star event rider. You thought your mother would live to hold your baby daughter in her arms."

The word choice was so direct, so surgical, I felt as if I had fallen off at the top of a fence and the breath was forced from me as I hit the ground. Turning, I left the arena.

As I was walking toward the house, I realized I didn't have a bedroom anymore. Jules's sister, Fifi, was staying there. All I had was the carriage house, and I didn't want to go there. Instead, I went to CB's stall and sat on his hay. Since he was still outside until lunch, he hadn't had a chance to inhale it yet.

For the longest time I tried to decide if Lockie was being deliberately harsh, or if the words had just fallen from his lips without thought. It was such a painful image to envision. My mother and her granddaughter. There was no do-over, or repair in the way we had managed with my father. All opportunities had died with her. I had thought I was over the worst of these thoughts but Lockie knew exactly where to go for maximum effect.

The stall door slid open and he sat next to me.

I felt the tears filling my eyes then spilling down my face.

He put his hand on my knee.

***

Greer, Lockie, Jules, and I were having lunch when Fifi shuffled into the kitchen with her hair uncombed and wearing an over-sized tee shirt and boxers.

"Do you people get up this early every morning?" Fifi said with a yawn, and she tried to find the coffee.

"It's noon. This is lunch and there's no coffee," Jules replied. "I would appreciate if you would come downstairs with clothes on."

Fifi glanced down. "I'm wearing clothes."

"Street clothes, then," Jules replied sharply. "The kind you can't see through."

She began opening cabinet doors looking for something. "What?"

"This is not your family. You're a guest in the house and I'm sure none of us want to see you semi-naked."

Fifi laughed. "What a quaint idea. Everyone wants to see me naked."

Greer picked up her plate and left the table with Joly following behind her.

Tightly coiled, Jules seemed to be on the verge of throwing something.

"It's okay, Jules, I don't have X-ray vision. I didn't even look," Lockie said.

The kitchen door opened and Cam entered. It took a moment for him to understand the scene.

"What the..."

"This is Jules's sister, Fifi," I said.

"Of course it is," he replied, unhappily. "Buck shouldn't be exposed to this much exposure. I'll take him to Acadiana. My mother will be here in a while. Don't let her in the house."

Cam left the kitchen.

Fifi leaned up against the countertop and shrugged. "The Puritans are alive and well in New England."

"There's room at the Inn," I said. "Go there. I need my bedroom."

"Talia?" Lockie asked.

"Where's the coffee, Jules?" Fifi asked, impatiently.

"This isn't a diner. We don't have coffee all day long. At the Inn, you can have coffee anytime. Sleep all day, stay up all night."

"Like there's anything to do in this deadbeat town at night," Fifi shot back.

"Then go home," Jules suggested.

"You know I can't do that."

"Go to Rome. Go to Paris. Go to Tahiti. Newbury, Connecticut is hardly your speed."

"There's a speed to this antiquated village?"

Fifi left the kitchen and went upstairs to my bedroom. It made me wish I hadn't been so generous.

Jules placed her napkin on the table. "Excuse me." She left the kitchen.

I sighed.

"Tal, are you moving out of the carriage house?"

I turned to Lockie. "What? No. I just want her off the farm. She's too...and I don't want a naked woman parading around in front of you."

"She wasn't naked."

"You said you didn't look."

"I gave her a cursory glance. Wow. That was enough!" He reached over and put his hand on mine. "I'm teasing. I looked. That's what guys do."

"She made it impossible not to," I said.

"That's the point." Lockie stood. "Women like Fifi are like a neon sign with no off switch. They're constantly advertising." He brought our plates to the sink and I brought the glasses.

"She's pretty," I replied.

Lockie opened the freezer door. "We have twenty minutes before the afternoon starts. What do I have to do to persuade you to go to the pond and have an ice cream cone?"

"Ask."

He put the ice cream on the counter then nuzzled his face against my neck. "Sit with me and we'll let ice cream melt over us."

"That's the best offer I've had all day. I'll bring the wipes."

***

9

We put Cap up on Spare and sent her out to ride in Day's lesson instead of staying in the apartment to do a slash and burn destruction of everything belonging to Mill. I finally persuaded her to see the wisdom in keeping things even if he had touched them because I knew that eventually the disappointment would fade and there was a chance she'd want them.

Without hearing his explanation, Mill's decision was surprising. Assuming there was no one else for him, why wouldn't Mill continue the relationship? As far as I knew, Cap had never complained about the separation. Not being the clingy, needy type, I didn't think she wanted more from Mill.

Having Lockie riding the circuit in Europe would be very difficult for me, but I wouldn't think of breaking up. Lockie might. If he had no idea when he was coming home, he might construe it as a favor to me to square dance with someone else in my spare time.

People do change their minds. What initially seems like a good idea in theory can fall apart in practice. I hoped that was the case for Cap and Mill. If not, she still needed to keep her life moving forward and Spare was part of that.

While acting as ground crew, I paid attention to everything Lockie said, not as a rider but as someone who had students. A session with him was so different than any instructor I'd had in the past. On a different level, it became an intellectual exercise. Lockie thought about the horse and rider then the work of the day reflected the specific needs.

I could only think of the torture we went through as each trainer attempted to mold us into some ridiculous ideal when Greer and I had our own issues. They never looked at us, and they never saw us as individuals, just as junior eq riders. Until Lockie had arrived at the farm, we fit the program, the program didn't fit us.

I didn't want to be the kind of trainer who became caught up in the end results while forgetting that each day's good ride was the goal.

Perhaps feeling me watching him, Lockie turned to me, and smiled.

And he said he was lucky.

***

We squeezed together on the chaise lounge on our back terrace and watched the sun lower behind the hills.

"I'm sorry I upset you this morning," Lockie said.

"I'm sorry I had unkind thoughts about you," I replied.

"What? Go back and explain that."

"My first reaction was that you said it on purpose."

"Why would I intentionally hurt you?"

I took a breath. "Not to hurt but to accept."

Lockie squeezed me. "You credit me with more wisdom than I possess but thank you."

I kissed his cheek knowing the truth.

"How closely did you look at Fifi again?"

"Talia, I studied her right down to the little mole on her upper thigh."

I sighed.

"She has nice legs. The problem with riders is that your muscles conform to the sides of the horse. They flatten out. Fifi's legs...shaped like Miss America's. Or...who are those girls with the wings?"

"I don't know."

"Sure you do, the famous models wearing their thongs and cantilevered bras. Click. Click. Click with the cameras."

"I'm sorry I asked."

Lockie laughed.

2

I WAS IN GREER'S OFFICE, reviewing the schedule when Lockie opened the door.

"Tal, Mauritz has an opening at eleven. If I leave now, I can make it. May I take CB?"

"Why are you asking?"

"He's your horse."

"You don't have to ask."

"I'm going to say 'Tal, I'm taking your horse to my dressage lesson'?"

"Yes."

Greer sighed loudly enough for everyone in the barn to hear.

"I'm not doing that," Lockie replied.

"Okay. Take him."

"Are you coming with me?"

"No," I said. "Just the two of you. Do some male bonding. Stop at Pickett's Pub and have a beer and a veggie burger on the way home."

"I don't have time to argue with you," Lockie said.

"That's the last thing I want to do with you."

"What's the first?" he asked.

We looked at each other for a moment. "Bye. Who is taking over your lesson with Nicole?"

"Cam." Lockie started out the door.

"Hah," Greer replied.

He paused. "Yes, and someone chaperon them, okay?"

"She's hot to trot," I quipped to Greer.

"Is it called trotting now?" Greer asked.

"Yeah. Okay. Just make sure someone is on the ground with Cam and I'll see you in a few hours." Lockie disappeared into the barn.

"Send Freddi out there," Greer said. "Cap's taking the afternoon off to visit some friends in Old Newbury."

"I don't blame her," I replied.

"This is what happens to you when you get involved with boys."

"Can happen," I admitted. "She could have been the one to end it. Cap could be the one who made Mill crazy."

Greer gave me her special, patrician glare designed to stop anyone in their tracks. "I understand what you're not saying, and I encourage you to not say it."

"Sometimes it's good to hear what you don't want to hear."

"He'll get past it," she replied.

"I think you're wrong."

"Talia..."

"What's the worst that could happen?"

"Kate's actor friend has found a summer rental on Oser Pond and the daughter, Ami, is going to spend the summer riding here. What pony are you going to put her on?"

"There are only two choices. Call or Fudge. Has she ever ridden before?"

"She goes to Deacons Hall School and they have a good riding program," Greer replied, then paused. "We live with our horses. Most people don't do that anymore."

"True. So?"

"Let's just be mindful of that reality."

"We force Nicole to do the work when she's here but she has no emotional connection to Obi. How are we going to instill that into her?"

Greer shook her head.

"Maybe it can't be done. Maybe that's just her. Cold."

I had been wondering about Nicole and how she would fit into our program. So spoiled by having grooms to do everything for her and a trainer who had much invested in her besides time, she had no idea there was work involved in having a horse. She didn't want to know. There was a force field of denial around her and nothing we said got through.

Still, to have Nicole riding at the farm was a nice boost financially and she was good publicity. Nicole was a winning rider who got her picture in *The Equestrian Gazetteer*, which meant Bittersweet Farm was also mentioned. Lockie was identified as her trainer. She had friends who wanted to ride and wanted new horses, and we had already started to see her positive impact on the farm.

We had also seen the negative impact. She was impatient, petulant, and lazy. Easily distracted by her social life, her work ethic was almost nonexistent. She felt she knew how to ride well enough to win, and that was all that was important. Nicole cared about her horse for what it could do for her but not as a partner.

Fortunately, for Obilot, we all adored her and she didn't lack for attention.

I hoped Cam would take Nicole aside and say something to her, but, of course, he didn't want to do that because a personal chat could be perceived as encouragement.

"Let's focus on what we can do. Day invited us to ride their property as practice for the outside course classes at Miry Brook. When do you want to go?" Greer asked.

"Who are we bringing?"

"Pavel can drive the van, and we can take the trailers. I think it's good for the pony riders."

"Definitely. Tomorrow is as good a day as any."

"Will Lockie want to go?" Greer wondered. "Who is he riding at the show?"

"I think Henry's going. We could ask Cam to come along just for the fun of it."

Cam would be a couple hundred miles away on the weekend of the Miry Brook show, riding Tropizienne for Teche Chartier. There was seventy-five thousand dollars in prize money at stake, so there was no question where the Acadiana horses would be.

"Buck would probably like that," Greer replied. "Ask Cam."

I wanted to suggest she ask him, but there was so little point in it. "Okay. Do you want to ride later this afternoon?"

"Sure."

I started for the door.

"Ask Cam if he wants to ride Counterpoint," she said evenly.

"At the Jamieson farm?"

"That and to take Whiskey's place."

"That's very kind of you," I replied.

She went back to her paperwork.

When I reached the house to have lunch, Jules was carrying two suitcases, and Fifi was carrying three bags out the door.

"I'll be back in twenty minutes. Either wait or put it together yourself. Everything is in the refrigerator."

Fifi looked over her shoulder at me as she was hurried along the walk. "She's putting me in Inn jail."

"The real jail is just down the street if you prefer authenticity," I told her, wondering what she had done to be bum-rushed away.

***

A half hour later, Jules returned and closed the door firmly behind her.

"I'm so sorry," she said.

I didn't want her apologizing for something that wasn't her fault. "Please, Jules, you've put up with so much from us this year. She's family. You wanted to help."

"No, I didn't! Fifi barged in without an invitation."

The door opened and Cam took a step inside. "Is the way clear?"

"She's gone."

"Perfetto," he replied, going to the sink to wash up. "When's Lockie getting back?"

"You're doing Nicole," I said.

Cam gave me a look.

"Her lesson," I added. "He forgot to mention it?"

Nodding, Cam dried his hands and went to his seat. "Where's Gracie?"

"Working with Amanda." I brought the salads to the table.

"Can we persuade her to ride in with Nicole?"

"Do you know what you're asking?"

Jules brought the sandwiches made with the brioche rolls she had baked earlier that morning and sat next to me.

"Yes." Cam reached for a sliced beef sandwich. "Pete Bouley found a house to rent for the summer, so Buck will be staying with him for the foreseeable future."

"I'm sorry. I know you enjoyed having him at your house."

"It was almost like the old days except I didn't hang him out the window like I did my brother, Ker." Cam smiled.

"You didn't," Jules said.

"Yes, I did. I am the evil middle child."

"And proud of it," I replied.

"Of course!"

The door opened and Greer entered followed by Joly.

"Where's Buck?" Cam asked.

"His father came for him, but he'll be back tomorrow to go to the Jamieson farm."

"What's going on there?"

"Day offered to let us ride the property as preparation for the Miry Brook show. I was going to get around to asking if you'd like to join us," I said, "but other news came first."

"If it's in the afternoon, yes."

"It has to be after school because of the pony riders," I replied.

"Gracie, would you ride in Nicole's lesson?" Cam asked, as she sat in her place.

"No."

I poured myself a glass of Jules' berry juice spritzer and kept my head down.

Cam spooned some chopped salad onto her plate. "Help me out."

There was silence.

"I'll make it up to you somehow," Cam added.

"No. You shouldn't have to pay me to do you a favor," Greer said. "I could ride Kyff."

I smiled at the thought of Nicole having to watch Greer easily ride a horse who had dumped her so publicly in Florida.

Greer took a sandwich and cut it in half. "Bria needs the work, though."

The door opened and Lockie came in.

I expected the worst. "What are you doing home so early?"

Plainly, he was upset. "Have you ever seen a horse go sideways?"

"Yes, they do it all the time. It's called a half-pass."

"No, that's a diagonal movement. Forward and to the side. CB was just going to the side. That was when he wasn't inventing new gaits. People came from the barn to watch. It was a real crowd pleaser. That and the caprioles."

Jules leaned over to me. "What's a capriole?"

"I don't know," I whispered back.

"It's when they jump into the air," Lockie replied.

"Do we need to get Dr. Fortier up here?" Greer asked. "He sounds sick to me."

"He sounds mental to me," Cam said.

"I have a headache. Can you cancel Nicole's lesson?"

"I've got it covered," Cam said.

"Thank you."

"Do you want me to—" I started.

"No." Lockie walked out of the house.

"Is he okay?" Jules asked.

Greer looked at me and I was sure we were both remembering the last time we raced him to the Emergency Room of the local hospital.

"Do you think the two events are related?" Cam asked.

"I was thinking the same thing," I replied. "Did he have the headache before or after the ride. If before, did CB sense it? If after, did CB cause it?"

"Or did he just get a headache," Greer said. "Don't complicate it."

I pushed back from the table. "I'll bring him a sandwich and check on him. If you could prepare for Nicole who will be here momentarily, I'll still be your ground crew."

"We can handle it." Cam held out the platter of sandwiches to me.

A few minutes later, I entered the carriage house to find Lockie sleeping on the leather sofa. I left the sandwich and a container of salad for him and went back to the barn.

***

Nicole wasn't happy to have Greer riding in her lesson but since she was still trying to impress Cam, she had to smile and accept the situation. Being so accustomed to riding equitation and junior hunters, Nicole was not comfortable with the suggestion she pick up the pace. We were treated to a long lecture from Nicole about her experience, the definition of expression and that hunters weren't jumpers. Lockie would not have listened to the rant but Cam let her finish, then said Obi needed more impulsion if Nicole expected to clear larger fences.

Riding Bria with complete control, Greer took the course following Cam's instructions and it made me realize how good Lockie had been as a trainer for both of us. The timing of his arrival had been perfect. Any earlier and Greer would never have listened to him. Once making it to the finals was impossible, the pressure was off and she could concentrate on what was important.

Cam finished the lesson with a good round for Nicole, reminded her of the issues she still needed to work on and then everyone left the ring.

With time before the pony riders were expected, I decided to go back to the carriage house and, upstairs, found Lockie in fresh clothes, hair wet from a shower.

"Hi," I said.

There was no reply.

I sat on the edge of the bed. "Is there anything I can do for you?"

"I don't need to be babied," Lockie said.

"Absolutely correct. We're going to the Jamieson farm tomorrow. Are you going? I need to know what vehicles we're taking."

"Why don't you say what you're here to say?"

"I just did. What do you think I want to say?"

"I did not provoke your horse. Don't take his side." Lockie put on his boots.

"Whatever happened at Balanced Rock is between you and CB."

"No, I didn't hit him."

"You've been here almost a year and I've never seen you angry with a horse. I'm sure that CB has tested your patience but going to war is not part of your training program." I stood. "I've got the ponies arriving so I'll see you later. There's a sandwich for you if you're hungry."

"I found it."

"Not to baby you, just to be courteous to someone I care about," I added.

There was a long silence.

"Something happens. I don't know that it's coming on. I have no awareness of it when it's happening and then it's like a switch is thrown and it's gone."

"Dr. Jarosz explained the injury and the ramifications to me. It must be very disorienting."

"It's embarrassing," Lockie replied.

"No. It's a miracle that you survived. You have some headaches, a few holes in your memory, and the movies are too loud for you. That's a small price to pay for your life."

"I'm not ungrateful."

"I never thought that."

"Knowing I'm not going to get better, this is what you want?"

I stepped closer, put my arms around him, and lay my head against his chest. "Oh yeah."

Lockie wrapped his arms around me. "Talia, he was spectacularly obstinate."

"You're just annoyed that he made you feel like a beginner."

He nuzzled my neck. "That's a normal response."

"He's testing you."

"I've been riding him for eight months."

I paused. "Every time you ask CB to move up a level in difficulty, you have a problem with him."

"Yes."

"You've said that the memory of the horse works as an asset to a good trainer and a liability to a bad one."

"Yes..."

"What if he's remembering how he was mistreated?"

"Do you want me to apologize to him?"

"Yes, by going back to the beginning. Start him over."

Lockie stepped away.

"It's up to you. If you see this as a challenge, accept it and work with CB on his terms. If you just want any dressage horse, find a new horse."

"I don't know."

"He doesn't want to be your ride, he wants you to be his partner."

Lockie leaned over and kissed me. "Stop being so smart."

3

I HAD JUST MOUNTED CB when Victoria rode up to me on Dice. A moment later, Greer came around the van on Tea.

"What are you doing here at Jamieson Farm?"

"Sibby invited me," Victoria said. "She says there was going to be a group having fun this afternoon."

"And you love to have fun," Greer replied.

"I do. Are you going to hold that against me?" Victoria asked.

"Yes." Greer turned Tea away and went to meet up with the Zuckerlumpens.

I was left with Victoria, not knowing what to say.

"I found Fifi Finzi at the Inn and invited her to stay at Rowe House."

"She doesn't get up until noon and has little interest in clothing, so as long as you know that, you'll probably enjoy having her around."

"She's very beautiful," Victoria said as we walked toward the group.

"There's no denying that."

"She would make a good Aria."

"Does she act?" I asked.

"Is that a requirement?"

"I don't know anything about such things but she has been given many free passes in her life just because she's so attractive."

"That's the curse women like that live with. Fifi is not more beautiful than Greer. She possesses a different kind of beauty," Victoria commented.

"Flashy. Greer is very reserved," I replied. "What Greer am I talking about?" I asked myself out loud.

"At the heart, Greer is a lady," Victoria said. "She surpasses me in deportment."

"I've never seen you dancing on a table holding an empty bottle of champagne, so you get high marks for that."

"Thank you, Talia. I'm sure it was difficult for you to find something positive to say about me."

"My mother hoped I would find the good in anyone. I don't always succeed."

"Sarah was a remarkable woman. Of course, I was very angry for a time, but I always did understand the choice. In many ways, I have what I've always wanted now. No family but a house and money of my own."

"It's possible to keep two balls in the air but never three," I said. "My mother had me and my father but not health."

"What are your two balls?" Victoria asked. "Lockie..."

"Yes. He's very important to me. The farm, my family, my students, but when I compare my efforts to Greer who is so accomplished and is so successful with her charity work, maybe my world is too narrow. Maybe I should be turning my attention to the Swope Foundation."

"Do you have time?"

"No, but I should be able to make time."

We walked in silence for a moment.

"I know you don't want to take advice from me but if you hadn't done the homeschooling option, you would have been graduating from high school this month. There is time ahead of you, Talia, to put all the pieces of your life together."

"There wasn't time for my mother."

"That's not your template. Your life will be different than Sarah's."

Poppy and Gincy trotted over to me, braids bouncing.

"Why are you such a slow-poke? It's time to leave!"

Riding beside me, Gincy's head came up to my knee and CB reached down with his nose to give Tango the once over.

"Sometimes the small things are the big things," Victoria said, then trotted away to catch up with Sibby.

"Let me explain this situation to you. Sibby is Day's grandmother and the master of the Newbury Hunt. Her word is law. Day said we're going to go the route where there are lower versions of the jump or you can go around. If either of you don't want to jump something, that's fine. Before either of you start crying out in the field, tell me and we'll quit. Okay?"

"Okay," they both replied.

The other riders were moving off. Greer was alongside Day. Lockie, Cam, and Buck were behind Sibby. Victoria was with Cap and Freddi. I held CB to a trot so the ponies could keep up at the beginning.

It was a beautiful old farm, much like ours, but the Jamiesons had been hunting over this land for close to a hundred years. The pastures were delineated by perfectly maintained stone-walls, not split rail fences.

If there was a family who better represented what the Miry Brook show was about, I hadn't heard about them. Connecticut history was surrounding us and their attic must have been like a museum. I wondered what outfit Day was going to wear for the retro classes because she must have decades of clothing to choose from.

We went up a rise and found a chicken coop appropriate for the horses, but far too much for the ponies. The open gate was our choice. We trotted through it as the distance between us and the field increased.

At the end of the field, we entered the woods and followed the trail. Poppy was cantering in the lead, Gincy was in the middle, and I was the last rider of the entire group.

There was a small log across the trail and the ponies had no trouble getting over that. The girls had spent a substantial amount of time on Lockie's cross-country course so there was no doubt in my mind that they would have trouble with anything here or at the show. The trip to Jamieson Farm was to reinforce the confidence they already had. Since the outside course at Miry Brook was being held on a flat field, Gincy didn't have the worry of cantering downhill, something that still concerned her unless I was nearby.

Poppy hand-galloped down the trail and CB was able to canter slowly behind them. We turned a corner and Lockie was waiting for us in a clearing.

"You were having such a hard time keeping up, they sent me back to find you," he said with a smile.

Poppy reached up to him and he was unsure for a moment, then took her hand.

"Thank you."

"You're very welcome," he replied. "Would you like to trade horses?"

Poppy giggled. "You're too tall for Tango!"

"Right you are. Henry will just have to trot."

"Can he make it over the big fences at a trot?" Gincy asked.

"Yes, he can. You'd be surprised at what he can do."

"Is he going to become a star?"

"I don't know, Gincy. It takes a lot of work to get your picture in *The Gazetteer*," Lockie replied.

"But you've had your picture in there," Poppy said.

"I have."

"What's that like?"

Lockie looked over her head to me and I shrugged.

"It's nice confirmation that you're riding well but it's not the only feedback you can get. What's more important is to judge for yourself how well you're doing and not rely on what a judge might say about what happens in one class."

"I don't know," Gincy replied. "If you don't win, aren't you failing?"

Lockie laughed. "You're only competing against yourself. One class or a year of classes is not the definition of who you are."

"It feels good to win," Poppy said.

"Yes, it does," I replied. "You challenged yourself and that day everything went in your favor. Some days everything doesn't. It's your attitude that really counts. That's your test. Tango would appreciate your good mood more than a blue ribbon."

Poppy patted his neck. "You'll tell me if..."

"You won't," I said, "but, yes, I will. How about we stop talking and start trotting?"

The ponies went out ahead of us.

Lockie leaned over. "Kiss me, Silly."

I leaned toward him. "They didn't really send you back."

"That was my idea."

"I like the way you think." I kissed him.

***

There were a half dozen cars parked in the driveway when Lockie turned the van off the road, one blocking the way. No one was in the driver's seat so I got out to check if there were keys in it.

I came back to the van and got up on the step. "No keys. There's a PRESS sticker on the windshield."

"I'll push it out of the way."

"With the van?"

"Yes."

"You'll crush the trunk."

"Okay."

"You can't."

"I have horses on here who want to get off."

"CB's been in there for fifteen minutes. He didn't start banging on the hull of the jet over the Atlantic on the way here from Germany."

"He was drugged."

"Are you serious?" I asked.

Lockie gave me a look.

"I'll run down to the house and find out what's going on." I hopped off the step.

"It's about Fifi!" he called after me.

As I trotted down the driveway, I wondered how it could be about Fifi. She didn't live with us anymore. Arriving at the terrace, I knew Lockie had been right. There were photographers and journalists trying to crowd around Jules while Pavel and Tomasz kept them back.

"For the last time! I don't know where my sister is!"

"She was here," someone called out.

"She left. How many times must I say it?"

"Did you know she was seeing Dubhlainn Quale?"

"I have no information about my sister, you'll have to ask her," Jules replied.

Dubhlainn Quale. He was the super hot Irish actor who had appeared in seemingly every movie I had seen last year. It was said he had the look of the ocean battering the Irish coast.

I thought he was married to Jilli Achor. So much for marriage vows among the celebrity elites.

Lockie was more handsome. It wasn't a secret but I almost wanted it to be. Not for my sake, but his. I knew how difficult life had been made for Greer by being beautiful. People reacted to the surface and she became invisible.

It was true for me, too. For many years, it was hard to see the Greer so plainly behind the veneer. Only Cam had managed the X-ray vision at first sight.

I hoped she would stay in the truck and avoid the predators, because they could turn to her in an instant. If they had done their homework, they would have to know Victoria *"Damned Desire"* Rowe's daughter lived here.

Approaching the crowd, I reminded myself they were journalists, not detectives. Fixated on Fifi, that's all they cared about. They wouldn't see me, or Greer, or Lockie. They were looking at a beautiful woman, Jules, and it hadn't registered at all.

I pushed through the bodies, looped my arm through Jules's and guided her into the house. "Sorry, scribes. This is private property. Move your cars before I call the police."

Pavel and Tomasz stationed themselves in front of the door.

"Where's Dad?" I asked, closing the door behind us.

"On his way up from the city but it's a long drive. He'll get here by dinner."

"Did you know Fifi is staying with Victoria now?"

Jules went to the refrigerator and removed a large platter of small cakes and tarts. "No. Where did you hear that?"

"Victoria was out riding with us," I replied.

"I didn't know she liked horses that much. Studs, yes. Horses, no."

I laughed.

"Let this be a lesson to you, Tal. Never overestimate the intelligence of an entertainment reporter," Jules said. "How hard would it be to find Fifi in a small town?"

"Fortunately, impossible."

"So far," Jules added.

I tried not to grin. "They have no idea what awaits them at Rowe House Farm."

"Victoria will be handing out free copies of her new book and relating the exploits in her life that gave her the material for the story."

"Embellished, of course."

Jules looked at me. "Really?"

"She may have a very vivid imagination."

"Why would you say that?"

"Dad. How could he be so wrong about her?"

Jules raised an eyebrow. "What's that theory?"

"She must have some redeeming qualities." I saw the van drive past the house. "The newshounds must have gotten out of the way. I should go help Lockie with the horses."

"Tal, I'm sorry about Fifi."

"Don't apologize for her."

"She must have some redeeming qualities?"

"You're wonderful and she's your sister, so yes." I opened the door. "We'll be up in about a half hour."

***

We took care of the horses and ponies, cleaned out the trailers and van, then did the afternoon chores. Day and the Zuckerlumpens left. Pete Bouley drove away with Buck after waiting for him at Jamieson's farm. I thought that was evidence he was trying and hoped Buck would give him a chance.

"Come up to the house and eat with us," I suggested to Cam, not wanting him to be so reminded that Buck wouldn't be at the Cooper's table any longer.

He looked at Greer before answering.

I liked that. I liked that she didn't tell him to grab a burger at the Grill Girl's.

"I'm filthy," he said.

"We all are," Lockie replied.

"Isn't it a rule that you clean up and change for dinner?" Cam asked.

"That was the rule," Greer sighed.

"We can't maintain that level of civility anymore," I said.

"Okay," Cam replied.

We started for the house.

"Are you coming, Cap?" I stopped walking when I saw she wasn't with the group.

"I have a date," she said.

We all froze.

"Terrific," I managed to say once my temporary paralysis passed.

Cap nodded and went down the aisle to her apartment.

"Who?" Greer asked.

"No idea," I replied. "Someone from around here?"

As we walked up the driveway, Mackay Berlin drove down toward the barn and gave us all a wave.

"There's your answer," Lockie said.

I noticed Cam was smiling.

4

"CAGE FIGHTING OR THE CUPCAKE BAKE-OFF,"
I called to Lockie in the bathroom.

"How can you ask?" he shouted back.

"I have bad news for you," I said.

He turned on the water. "What?"

"Bad news. I was kidding about the cage fighting."

The moment I dropped the television remote, his phone
started to ring.

"Lockie, your phone's ringing," I called loudly so he
could hear me over the water.

"Talia, I'm trying to take a shower."

"What do you want me to do?"

"Answer it!"

I didn't answer his phone. That was private. Maybe it was all business, but I wasn't sure. Everyone needs their space, although neither of us actually had any.

Picking it up, I hoped it would go to voice mail. When it didn't, I clicked it on. "Hello?"

"Is that you, Talia?"

"Yes."

"This is Sibby Jamieson."

"Hi. Thank you for having us all over to your farm. I think it helped my pony riders."

"You're welcome any time. Is Lockie around?"

"He'll be here in a couple minutes. Is there anything I can do for you?"

"My friend is on the committee of a local show and the judge they counted on for this weekend, will be in the hospital getting her ankle pinned back together. I thought Lockie might stand in. With his experience, he'd be perfect."

I agreed whole-heartedly. Lockie had done a few clinics and everyone had been pleased, judging a show would be a natural progression.

He came into the bedroom wearing a tee shirt and shorts. "Who's on the phone?"

"Sibby. She wants you to judge a show." I held the phone out to him."

He put the phone against his chest. "You know your riding career is over when they start asking you to judge."

"Don't be ridiculous," I replied.

"Hi, Sibby," he said into the phone.

I went to the bathroom to take my shower, trying to think of any riders who continued to have a career and judged simultaneously. Since I had paid so little attention to showing, judges and trainers until last year, I couldn't think of one but that didn't mean one didn't exist. It didn't mean that Lockie couldn't be the first.

As this past year had been a transitional period for Greer and me, so had it been for Lockie. We were all in other places with new goals. I had just wanted to graduate from high school and stop showing. Now I found myself teaching, and training.

Training riders was nothing new for Lockie. Being a judge seemed a natural extension. He would be commenting on their training but with prizes. I couldn't see how this opportunity was so radically different from what he had already been doing.

After dressing and returning to the bedroom, he was still on the phone, which told me he had accepted. I went downstairs to get the fruit salad Jules had sent home with us.

When I returned, he was in bed clicking the remote and the channels sped across the screen. "Which one has the cage fighting?"

I handed him the bowl of fruit. "None of them."

"Talia, you know the talking thing you want to do so persistently?"

"I refute the characterization of it as persistent, but, yes, I know the talking thing."

Lockie ate a piece of melon. "I would like to discuss the offer Sibby made."

"Didn't you already say yes?"

"No. I listened and took notes but wanted to talk to you before going forward."

I got into bed next to him. "What's your reluctance?"

He picked around the fruit searching for the blueberries.

"Is it really that you think some part of your life will be behind you if you say yes?"

"Is that foolish?"

"Help me to understand. You've been teaching since aging out of juniors. You give clinics, train, show. Give me a clue."

"Up until now, I've just been helping other riders. If I go down this road, then I'll be an authority."

I tried not to smile. "Lockie, you're already more experienced and knowledgeable than the rest of us."

He was silent.

"It's one local show."

"It always starts with the first step and then a year later, you see how you've deviated from the path you were on. It's been that way with me. I had time to think about it when I was in the hospital."

"When you started to be able to remember what you thought the day before."

He nodded. "I realized that decisions you just throw away are those that often change your life."

"Did you think for a very long time about coming here?"

"No. I didn't have a choice. It was the only offer I was going to get. For everyone, I was in the past. I was damaged goods. People talk."

"They do. They shouldn't."

"I took this because I didn't have anything left to sell but my truck and trailer."

"Coming here changed your life."

"Yes, it did," Lockie agreed.

"So?"

"Am I ready to take this step?"

"My grandmother says—"

"Swope or Margolin?" he asked.

"Swope. She says everything in your life is meant for you. If this is in your life, you must be ready to take the step. You aren't under any pressure to say yes but that's your choice."

"I'll sleep on it. What channel is the cage fighting on?" Lockie picked up the remote and started scrolling through the channels again.

"I was teasing you."

He stared at me. "Just when I thought you were starting to like me a little."

I reached for the remote. "Give it to me."

He held it off to the side.

"The cupcake challenge is on."

"Cupcake, you shouldn't have gotten my hopes up. Let's watch *Fight Club*."

"Who are you?"

"I'm the one with the remote," he reminded me.

The channels continued scrolling past at speed then the screen went black.

"You broke it."

"I shut it off. There's nothing on." The plastic rattled as he placed it on the nightstand, then turned off the light. "You're too far away, Silly."

I moved over so we were touching and he reached for my hand.

"Pretend it's tomorrow morning," Lockie said.

"Alright."

"I'll judge the show if you are my assistant."

"You could take Cap. She needs to take her mind off Mill."

"She looked like Mill was the last thing on her mind as she got ready for her date with Mackay."

"That was a surprise," I admitted. "She didn't mention it to me."

"They'll work it out."

"What do you mean they?"

There was no they any longer. There was Cap, and there was Mill and never the twain shall meet.

"They'll find their own separate paths. It has nothing to do with us. Are we going to the show or not?"

"Why?"

"It'll be good for you."

"Okay."

It would be good for me. That way, I could keep my eye on him all day, making sure he had water and took breaks in the shade.

"You're not going as my babysitter," he added.

"Am so."

Lockie squeezed my hand.

∽ 5 ∾

"I'VE GOT SOMEONE FROM THE COLLEGE coming here to interview me this morning."

I looked at Greer in surprise. "Isn't the school year over?"

"She wants to use it as a sample of her journalistic abilities as part of her resume."

More journalists. I'd had my fill this week.

"How does that help us?" I asked.

"It will appear in the campus paper and online."

"I hoped you would have time to ride with me."

"We usually go in the afternoon."

"But Lockie has gone to talk to someone from the show committee about judging this weekend and there are horses to exercise," I replied.

"All right. I'll ride as soon as the interview is over. She should be here any minute. Why don't you stay for it? You might have something to add."

"I doubt that you'll forget anything."

Greer shrugged and began neatening her desk.

"All Nicole can talk about is going away for the weekend with Cam."

"That's for your benefit," I replied.

"You do understand how easily things happen," Greer said.

"No, how easily could Cam succumb to the allure of Nicole?"

"He doesn't even need to like her. It'll be after a long day in the hot sun. They're jumping in the swimming pool. 'Oops. My top seems to have slipped off!' Cam swims over to check this event out. 'Cam, be a dear and retrieve it for me.' 'A body like yours shouldn't be covered up.'" Greer said as she put some manila folders in her desk drawer. "Biology will do the rest."

"No judgments. Is that a routine you pulled?"

"No, but I saw it done."

"Did it work?"

"It has a success rating of a hundred percent."

I shook my head. "Why would Cam choose Nicole over you?"

"Number one, I won't be there. This isn't about like, it's about sex. Miles from home."

"Say this did happen. Wouldn't she brag about it the first thing Monday morning?"

"Yes."

"And you would never talk to Cam again."

"Yes."

"Do you think he knows that?"

"It's about the spur of the moment. Biology takes over."

"No, Greer. He wouldn't do that. He wouldn't risk it."

"I'm hardly the only female in the horse world."

"You're the only Gracie."

"Talia, you're very nice but you don't have enough experience. Miss Right or Miss Right Now."

"Cam's not a guy. He's smarter than that."

The door opened and Cap entered followed by a thin, pale young woman with nondescript brown hair.

"Hi. I'm Nova Reeve. I'm here to see Greer Swope."

Greer stood and reached her hand out. "I'm Greer. It's very nice to meet you."

"See you later," Cap said and left the office.

"Have a seat." Greer gestured to a chair.

"Thanks. I saw the video. I didn't know such things still existed." Nova took a digital recorder out of her bag. "Is this okay? I can't take notes fast enough."

47

Greer nodded.

"What things still exist?" I asked.

"Side-saddle riding." Nova clicked on the device and put it on the desk.

"Yes, people still do it," Greer replied.

"Women people."

"I don't think that men ever rode side-saddle."

"But that would make sense, wouldn't it? Anatomical sense."

I looked at Greer.

She smiled. "Women didn't always ride side-saddle. In Geoffrey Chaucer's day, women rode astride."

"Then it became imperative to protect women," Nova said.

"What are you getting a degree in?" I asked.

Nova beamed. "Women's studies and journalism."

"You can't rewrite history," Greer replied. "You might wish it were different, and while you're entitled to your own opinions, you're not entitled to your own facts."

"I understand that, but what I don't understand, and what I'd like to explain to my audience, is why any woman would allow herself to be sexually subjugated in such a very antiquated and chauvinistic way today."

"Perhaps it's the same reason why the Society for Creative Anachronism exists," I said. "It's fun to dress up and pretend you live in another era. It's nothing more than that and some people enjoy it."

Nova shook her head in disbelief. "But this is so politically incorrect."

"To you," Greer replied.

"It's not a political statement," I added.

"Everything is political."

Greer pressed her lips together. "What would you like to know about the charity horse show being held at the Miry Brook Hunt Club?"

"Why would a modern woman sanction hunting?" Nova replied.

"I think this interview is over." Greer stood.

"Did you get everything you needed?" I asked.

Nova glanced from Greer to me, baffled. "You didn't answer any of my questions."

I crossed to the door and opened it.

"Nor will I," Greer replied.

I practically pushed Nova out into the aisle and followed right behind her to the broomstick she had flown in on.

"It's just another way men control women," she said, opening her car door.

"Give it a rest," I replied.

"You're probably one of those women who likes men."

I nodded. "I do. I'm crazy about them."

"You know you're a traitor to your kind."

"You don't seem to understand that we made an effort to avoid being as rude to you as you've been to us, but if you don't get off my property, I'm going to tell you exactly what I think of you, and I guarantee it won't be politically correct speech."

"I'll put that in the article," Nova snapped back at Greer and got in the car.

"Make sure you send us some complimentary copies." I turned and walked toward the upper barn.

Cam was on the aisle brushing the shavings off Jetzt.

"You're here early," I said.

"I was at Acadiana at six to help load the horses. Obi went. Nicole is supposed to get herself there and I have to be there by four to coach her for her hunter class." Cam straightened up. "I can't tell you how many times I had a coach with me at a show. You could probably count them on one hand. I managed."

"You're hardly the norm."

He looked at me. "Is that good or bad?"

"Good. When were you going to leave?"

"I was going to have lunch, ride Jetzt and leave."

"Could you do me a favor?"

"Of course."

"Take Greer to lunch in town. Grill Girl or Antonio's, it doesn't matter."

"Why would I do that?"

"She didn't have a good morning and I think she needs you."

Cam went back to brushing the gelding. "I can't imagine that."

"One of you has to make the effort and she's not going to be the one."

"I thought Lockie told you to—"

"Mind my own business?"

"I would have found a slicker way to say it than that but yes."

"My sister is my business. I'm just suggesting lunch. You said you were going to eat then ride. Come up with an excuse. I'm sure you'll think of something."

"Why do I need an excuse to ask Greer to lunch?"

"So you don't scare her off."

Cam laughed.

"What's so funny?" Greer asked coming into the barn.

"Have lunch with me, Gracie. I'll tell you all about my morning and you can tell me all about yours."

"How men should be the ones riding side-saddle?"

Cam grinned and nodded to me.

"No, thank you. I don't want to have lunch with a complete stranger," Greer replied.

"I'm not a complete stranger. I may be a partial stranger, we could fix that."

"You could go and bring something back," I suggested.

Greer thought for a moment. "I suppose."

Cam handed me the brush and followed Greer down the aisle. "I've never met anyone so reluctant to spend an hour with me."

"Your right leg is your anchor," Greer said.

Cam had put Greer's side-saddle on Jetzt, mounted and was walking around the ring for his first lesson.

"Like pliers?" he asked.

"But you don't lift your left leg otherwise you'd be losing your stirrup constantly and you need that platform."

"Got it."

Cam used the one leg near Jetzt's side and urged him into a trot.

"Did I tell you to trot?" Greer asked.

"No."

"I wasn't finished explaining the basics."

"I know the basics. Stay on."

A moment later, Jetzt was cantering easily around the ring and Cam was staying on with no difficulty.

Lockie came up behind me. "What's going on?"

"Cam is making a point," Cap replied.

Jetzt came through the diagonal, did a flying change, and went in the opposite direction when he reached the track.

"He's so good," Day commented, leaning against the rail.

"It's almost like he had ridden side-saddle before," Cap replied. "But we're smarter than that."

Hearing a car, I turned to see Aly Beck drive into the yard, park, and the Zuckerlumpens jumped out. Poppy ran over to me and stood on the bottom rail of the fence.

"What's Cam doing?"

"Having his first side-saddle lesson," Cap replied, then turned and went to the barn to help prepare the ponies for their ride.

"Boys don't ride side-saddle," Poppy said.

"That's right," Lockie agreed, and walked away.

"I think I have the flat part down. How do you jump?"

"Keep your right toe pointed down—"

"Greer. Seriously?"

"Why ask if you don't want me to tell you?"

"Toe down, then..."

"You roll forward onto your right thigh. Left shoulder to Jetzt's right ear. Make sure you have plenty of release with your reins and hold the position on landing."

Cam cantered toward the roll top and cleared it easily. They continued around the ring taking the lower fences then he came back to Greer, halted, and jumped off.

"Thanks, Gracie. Good lesson. You finish up with him because I have to get on the road."

He put his too big helmet on her head and boosted her into the saddle.

"Too bad there isn't a for-men-only side-saddle class at Miry Brook. I'd consider entering."

Gincy and Poppy giggled, then, when Cam winked at them on the way out of the ring, they nearly swooned.

"Go get your ponies ready for your lesson," I said.

"Bye, Cam!"

"Bye," he said as they ran across the yard. "I wish all girls were as easy to please."

Greer rode up behind him. "They are."

"The burden of proof is on you, Gracie. I'll see you on Sunday."

6

THE FAIRGROUNDS LOOKED FAMILIAR, and they should have since Greer and I had shown there a number of times when we were just starting out. Then our next trainer du jour began entering us in the smaller rated shows locally where everyone had better outfits and more expensive horses. There were no wooly, unshed horses in those early spring shows held at the fairgrounds.

Lockie and I arrived, found the head of the show committee, and were introduced to the volunteers. Everyone was either still in a good mood or annoyed that their feet were wet from the dew on the grass. I had my half-wellies on, Lockie had tall wellies and we would change when the sun dried the dew.

A volunteer brought us containers of tea and donuts made in a food truck parked near the show tent.

"It was so kind of you to fill in on such short notice," she said. "My daughter has been looking forward to this show all spring and would have been so disappointed if it had been cancelled. I won't tell you which rider she is."

"Good," Lockie replied. "My good opinion can't be bought by a donut or even a sandwich at lunch."

She laughed. "Judge humor. Got it. If you need anything, let me know. I'll see you later."

"Do you understand the form?"

We had been given a tablet set up with templates for each class, listing the entrants. I thought that was a terrific help. Spaces were provided for all the judging notations or comments Lockie wanted to make. He had entrusted me with this task in order to be free to concentrate on the galloping herd that would soon be entering the ring.

I finished my tea and looked at my watch. Ten minutes. Horses and ponies were being hurried back and forth, trainers were running from the warm-up area, mothers were carrying rags and carrots. It was a normal morning.

"We're here to help," Lockie said as we walked into the middle of the ring.

"Of course."

"Judges..."

"I know. I've seen some judges' cards." I looked at the first form. It was just a list of numbers, but I knew how hopeful they all were. "How quickly will you be able to pin the class?"

"I'll have a good idea when they enter the ring."

"Before they ride?"

"Can't you tell?"

There was no point in pretending to be that smart. "Certainly I can pick out the ones who won't be pinned," I replied.

"You know the rest, too," Lockie assured me.

A minute later, so many children entered the ring, it was nearly impossible to see the ponies hidden behind the horses and the rider who were taking the inside track obscuring the view of the riders on the rail. I almost shuddered and vowed I was never going to judge anything for as long as I lived.

It was like Wild Bill Cody chasing after the buffalos or at least the Oklahoma land grab. Riders were everywhere at speeds from zero to sixty while dropping stirrups and reins and going out of control. Shouts of "Inside!" and "Heads UP!" could be heard over the thundering hooves.

"I want to go home," I said in Lockie's ear.

"You're stuck for the day," he replied. "What's that kid's number on the white horse?"

"The white horse with the green stains on its hocks?"

"That one."

"Fifty-nine."

"She's saying something to the trainer every time she goes past. Can you tell what it is?"

I watched carefully. "Yes. She's saying 'help'."

"Go ask the ringmaster to have everyone halt, then go up to her and ask if she'd like to leave."

A minute later almost all the horses were almost entirely halted and the little girl was being guided from the ring.

"Madame Mertzola predicts tennis lessons in number fifty-nine's future," I said as the stampede resumed.

By lunchtime, we had seen ponies running out of even plain rail fences in the hunter classes and small children crying when they fell off. These kids made Gincy and Poppy look like Olympic hopefuls and I felt so bad for them.

There were about eight riders who consistently got pinned. Two of them could have gone to a different show if their horses were a bit fancier. They were definitely undermounted, but horses were expensive and not everyone could afford a mount for each level they reached.

Some riders shouldn't have been on the grounds at all. They weren't ready for a show even at this level but the trainers were probably bringing everyone at the barn and no one wanted to be left out. The feeling could well have been that everyone has to start somewhere. These kids should have started in about six months so they could have a good experience. I could only hope they were having fun.

I certainly hadn't been.

"Is this making you reconsider going to Miry Brook," Lockie asked between classes.

"No. I'm not taking that seriously."

"Good."

"I've got the best horse and the best trainer."

"I'm not sure about either of those assets," he said.

"I'm not riding him again until the show, so you'd better get your butt into his saddle."

"You can't not ride him until the end of June."

"Sure I can."

Another wave of riders began entering the ring.

I was serious about not riding CB. Lockie needed to work on his relationship with him, and if I kept intruding, they wouldn't be forced to work out their issues.

I handed Lockie a bottle of water and he took a drink.

"Thank you," I said.

"Isn't that what I'm supposed to say to you?"

"Is it?"

"If I remember rightly," he replied. "Number 16. NW."

NW—Needs work.

At the end of the show, riders would crowd around and ask Lockie why they weren't pinned. Their feelings would be hurt, and they would be terribly disappointed. They tried to do their best. At least most of them had.

NW was the most common comment he was making. It was true for nearly everyone on the grounds. The specifics weren't important to us, although they definitely were to the riders. They weren't ready to show yet, or were a half a year away from being able to win a ribbon. It took work. Most of these riders weren't putting in the time or their trainers weren't insisting upon it.

Or there was the thought I didn't want to consider, maybe their trainers just didn't know any better. Just because someone called themselves a trainer didn't mean they were an expert. It didn't even mean they had ridden with anyone who knew more than they currently did. I had seen that situation often when Greer and I were showing continually. Some trainers were more like well-paid nannies, taking their charges to the shows on the weekend and reminding them to keep their heads up, heels down.

That was fine up to a point but when the end result was a Nicole Boisvert, who had been riding for at least ten years and didn't know much beyond keeping the perfect position, it was fraud plain and simple.

The worst part was that most people didn't realize how little they knew. Until Lockie had arrived, I had suspected there was more to riding than we were being told, but we got by, and I didn't care.

Lockie made us care by being a good example, and by being an extraordinary trainer. The past months hadn't been a crash course, they had been an intensive. It was like pouring water onto the desert and every word he said disappeared into us.

Every day I learned something from him. I tried to be as good a trainer for my Zuckerlumpens as he was to us.

Gincy and Poppy would be ready to compete in the classes they were entered in at Miry Brook. They were going in Pony Hunters. Three classes each. That was plenty for the day and they could do what was required. Depending on the competition, they might not place at all. The important part, for me, was that they wouldn't embarrass themselves or their mounts.

If I ever saw either of them crying at the end of the day because they didn't win a ribbon, I would put an end to showing until that issue was resolved. I never wanted them to go up to a judge desperate to know what they had done wrong. They should know without being told. Being aware was part of the process.

I knew I was so lucky with Poppy and Gincy. Having two better pony riders was hard to imagine. They loved their ponies first. They had fun. They were sweet and cooperative.

Someday I would have a Nicole Boisvert. I was not looking forward to that day.

We left the ring as the ringmaster entered with the championship ribbons and trophy. Number forty-seven deserved the championship and she deserved to move up to the next level. I hoped the adults in her life would recognize that reality.

The tablet was handed over to the secretary and Lockie was thanked profusely by the show committee. Then he was asked to judge again later in the summer. He said he would be happy to if his schedule permitted it, which was a very nice way of saying no.

Before we could make our escape, we were surrounded by little girls in grubby jodphurs who had been sneezed on, rubbed on, and who had sat on tack all day that hadn't been cleaned properly.

"Why didn't I get pinned?" A small girl asked. "We got the correct lead and everything."

I didn't remember her. If I had seen the pony again, I probably would be reminded.

"I know you were all trying your best, and you're disappointed. Not winning is an indication that you need to go home and work harder. Practice produces results. You will become a better rider the more time you put in the saddle."

"What should we practice if you won't tell us what we did wrong?" another girl asked.

"Did you pick up the correct diagonal the first time? Did you get the correct canter lead from a walk without trotting into it? Were you sitting up straight, eyes forward, heels down? Did your pony scramble over the fences or did you see your distances between jumps. If you're honest with yourself, you don't need me to tell you what you need to work on." Lockie smiled. "Be happy. No one fell off and broke anything. Did you have a good time riding your horse? That's important."

They nodded.

"Believe me, a year from now you won't remember this show."

They looked at him in disbelief.

Some of them would remember. Some of them would go home and use their diaries to write in great detail about everything that had occurred at this show. They would obsess over it. Some had parents who would obsess over it.

"Ride without stirrups or bareback. Be stuck like glue to your horse and most of all, have fun this summer," Lockie told them.

Most of the girls thanked him and then walked away.

"They didn't believe me," he said as we went to the truck.

"Some did. It's hard for them. It's all about performing well and if you don't, you're a failure."

"I never felt that way," he admitted as we opened the doors and got in.

"Maybe that's why you were so successful."

"I wasn't that successful."

I laughed.

"I was until I aged out. Anyone who does anything well when they're young, is considered a prodigy. When you become an adult, you have to prove it wasn't a fluke."

I steered the truck toward the exit. "And you did."

"Sometimes it seems like it. It's a moving target. People I rode with this winter would say today that this proves the best I can do is judge backyard shows."

"Those people are vile. You don't believe that."

"I don't. I'm happy where I am. Don't think otherwise."

"I don't want you to wake up one morning and think you've been wasting your time, that you should have done something else."

"Like?"

"Went back to Germany. Rode Grand Prix."

"Show jumpers or dressage?"

"Either. I'm serious. I want the best for you."

"I have the best. Except for the Grand Prix dressage horse." Lockie paused. "I'll be serious, too. None of this is how I envisioned my life would be. It's better. I'm not worried about CB and if he'll ever cooperate. There's time. I never felt I had that luxury before. The demands never stop when you're riding at the upper levels. The accident was life's way of telling me to slow down. I'm grateful. So it's all good. I'm going to sleep off that nightmare of a horse show now."

The next time I looked at him, Lockie was asleep.

7

HE WAS SO TIRED when we arrived at the farm, that I left him at the house and did the afternoon chores without him. Jules packed me the market basket full of a watermelon salad, a variety of cheeses, fresh bread, cold roast chicken and chocolate cannolis for dessert.

We sat on the terrace. I ate, he picked.

"Too much standing in the sun?" I asked.

"Could be." Lockie stood.

"Get into bed and watch *Fast and Nefarious: Amarillo Drift*."

"Why would I do that? You'll come up and make me switch to *The Creampuff Wars*. What yucky thing can they stuff into pat a shoe this week? Stay tuned for the competition. You won't believe what they do with squid ink!"

"I promise I won't." Laughing, I followed him into the house and began putting the leftovers away.

There was a knock at the door and Lockie opened it to Greer.

"Hi. Am I interrupting anything?"

"Not at all," Lockie said as he gave me a quick kiss on the cheek and headed up the stairs.

"The show was too much?" Greer asked.

"Borderline. Are you here for a crisis or did you just want some company?"

"Company. I won't keep you long."

I opened the door to the terrace. "Lockie will be asleep in three minutes. If he wakes and needs anything, I'm here."

"Don't take this wrong," Greer said, following me outside. "Your mother was good practice."

"I've thought the same thing myself."

We sat in the chairs facing the pasture. Henry and CB were closer to the fence, and Bria was further up the rise.

"How was the show?"

"Standing in the middle of the ring is like having a Wild West show going on around you. It's going to give me nightmares for weeks."

"Did it remind you of us?"

"Of course."

"Me, especially," Greer replied.

"Us. Everyone is the same from the ground with the swirling of horses around."

"You didn't want to be there," Greer pointed out.

"Neither did you."

"I thought it would get me what I wanted. No. What I needed." Greer was silent for a long moment. "I've thought many wrong things in my still short life."

"Not many, a few."

"That's what I want to talk about," she said.

"Okay."

"Cam."

"What do you want to do?" I asked.

"My role model is my mother. Dad never lived with us."

"I know."

"Then I see you with Lockie. How did you do that?" Greer asked.

"I care about him more than I care about me. I don't want the lecture."

"I wouldn't do that."

"Life is short and unpredictable. My mother was supposed to help me pick out my wedding dress. I can't try to avoid being hurt by not living my life. Every moment is precious and not repeatable."

"This sounds so good in theory."

"It's not a theory, it's reality."

Greer sighed. "I want what Kate and Fitch have. Kate met him when she was our age and there was never anyone else."

"These are decisions. There has to be something in you that overrides impulses."

"You mean like traveling and spending the night with someone else."

"That would be one example," I said. "Giving up. Stop trying. Sometimes quitting seems so appealing, doesn't it? In those last months with my mother, there were moments I just didn't want to do it anymore. It was so difficult. Then I'd think about how much she had given me. The world seems to be about putting yourself first. You never have a genuine connection that way. You have to serve someone else. You must want to or it's not coming from the right motivation."

Greer fiddled with the potted geranium on the table. "What if that's not what Cam wants? Did you have this conversation with Lockie?"

"Not in these words but similar ones. Do you have feelings for Cam?"

"I never had real feelings for anyone before you. I was just angry with Dad. I didn't know him. I didn't know anyone."

"I didn't know him either. Now I understand why my mother loved him."

"He's a little bit baffled by us."

I laughed. "That's an accurate assessment of the situation. He tries so hard. You have to love him for that."

"I do." Greer stood.

"Do you feel any better?"

"I don't know what to do."

"Here's an idea. Why don't you let Cam make the move and then go along with it?"

"When have I ever let anyone drive my car?"

I stood. "Never and what has it gotten you?"

"There is a certain satisfaction in knowing you're independent."

"You can't be both, Greer. You can't be fully in a relationship and independent, too. It doesn't work that way no matter what anyone says."

"It could."

"Ask Kate if it can be done. Ask your mother."

Greer looked at me as if I had gone crazy. "My mother doesn't know anything about being in a long-term relationship."

"Exactly."

"You're done for the day. Go be with Lockie. On Monday I have an interview for the show."

"Another one? Cancel."

"No, I think they'll be okay. She's from asidenotastride dot com. There won't be any lectures on how I'm being a traitor to my kind." Greer paused on her way to the driveway. "If I knew what kind I am."

69

"You never looked good in labels," I called to her.

***

We had an easy day of trail riding, and an impromptu picnic by the pond. Cap helped Jules prepare the food, and was smiling for a change. She seemed to have put Mill out of her mind for the afternoon. Maybe Mackay had helped by taking her to dinner and the Thaden Theater to see a movie I'd never heard of. If anyone could put this emotional speed bump behind her, it was Cap.

During the meal, my father received three phone calls that he took with a shake of his head and a silent apology. The question of whether he would enter the political arena as a candidate had not yet been decided, but the deadline was drawing closer.

I thought he would tell us on the Fourth of July. That was timely and his associates would be at the farm. Greer and I hadn't discussed the possibility, but doubted it was the direction she wanted the family to take. After not growing up with our father, I wanted him home. Maybe that was selfish, but knowing what little I did of politics, I couldn't see how being in office would be any better than doing what he had been doing for all of my life. He had worked freely from the outside, to educate and inform people. This was his strength, and I wanted him to stay the course. I thought that's what my mother would have told him to do.

Of course, it wasn't my decision to make. We would all support him and work with him no matter what he chose. I did wonder about the skeletons in each of our closets that could be used against him by the political pundits or the opposition.

I helped clear the table then Jules and Cap served homemade strawberry gelato that was so good everyone had seconds and they weren't small portions.

Just as I was dragging my spoon through the bowl to get the last few drops, Cam's truck and trailer went down the drive and stopped in front of the barn. We went down to greet him and he was already walking Obi down the ramp.

"Where's Nicole?" I asked.

"As if she's going to be with her horse," Greer replied.

"It's not her horse, it's my horse," Cam said.

"Why is Obi your horse this afternoon?" Greer asked. When she left the farm, she was Nicole's horse."

"I won the Hunter Derby. Nicole didn't get pinned, threw a fit and I gave her the check. She didn't want the horse after this embarrassment. And Lockie, she says you're a lousy trainer."

"All evidence to the contrary," I replied.

Lockie shrugged.

"She's a lousy rider," Greer said. "Obi is, again, more horse than she can handle."

"Apparently the only horse she can ride is Mallard Chick."

"And fortunately, he went to someone who actually cares about him," Cap added.

Cam handed Freddi the lead shank.

"What are you going to do with Obi?" I asked.

"Ride her in the hunter division. She's a very talented mare. It wasn't her fault she didn't place in the hunter derby. Nicole was practically sitting on her neck. When she was here and being watched, she made the effort to follow instructions. Away from the farm, she reverted back to all her junior division habits. That worked then, but she was riding against some excellent competition and they were thinking. Nicole doesn't think when she rides, she poses. Sending the judge a note saying 'I do for blue' is not enough now."

"What?" I asked.

"Let it go," Lockie said. "She's history."

"Are you serious?" Greer asked.

"You never heard that?" Cam replied walking Jetzt out of the trailer.

"No."

"It's just gossip," Lockie said.

"Do judges take advantage of offers like that?" Greer demanded.

Lockie and Cam exchanged a look.

"Not that I've ever heard," Lockie said.

"You couldn't prove it by me," Cam agreed.

"It would make so much sense," Greer replied. "All this time I thought she was somehow a better rider than I was. I couldn't beat her no matter how hard I tried. Obviously, I wasn't trying the right things."

"Gracie—"

"It's cheating! As bad as I was, I never cheated. I was stupid but I was never cheap. For a blue ribbon?"

"We've all made bad choices," Cam replied, standing on the ground with Jetzt.

"Not Talia!"

"Leave me out of it," I said.

"You've done everything right!" Greer insisted.

"Okay. Let's pretend I've done everything right. So what? I had my issues to deal with and you had yours. You have Victoria as a mother and I had my mother. I don't want to feel guilty about it."

"Why should you feel guilty?" Greer demanded.

"Because you suffered so much and I wasn't smart enough to know what you were going through."

"Ding. Ding. Ding. Go to your own corners. We're not bringing up something that happened years ago," Lockie started.

"Don't say life isn't fair. I know it isn't fair. It's not about Nicole, and what she offered. It's that judges took her up on the offer. Is everyone so amoral?"

73

"Not everyone," I said. "We live in an imperfect world. You can only depend on yourself and the small circle around you."

"You cannot depend on me," Greer said.

"You can't tell me what to do," Cam replied. "If I want to depend on you, I'll damn well do it." He led Jetzt into the upper barn.

"I have to find something to do to get me out of this conversation," Lockie said leaving for the barn.

I looped my arm through Greer's and started for the house. "You need to forgive yourself for your mistakes. You do so much good now."

"I behaved like Nicole."

"Sometimes. Not anymore."

"Cam saw the way Nicole acted at the show and he thought of me."

I pulled her around and practically dragged her back to Jetzt's stall.

"Cam."

He looked up.

"Sshh," Greer hissed at me.

I tightened my grip on her hand so she couldn't bolt. "When you were at the show and Nicole threw her temper tantrum, did that remind you of Greer?"

"No."

"But..." Greer started.

"But nothing."

"Another time, maybe. How about in Napier," Greer asked.

"What are you trying to find out?" Cam stepped out of the stall and closed the door.

"Humor her," I suggested.

Cam raised his hands. "You don't remind me of anyone because I've never met anyone like you. Okay? It's been a long weekend and I'm going home."

Cam walked to the doorway and went into the stableyard.

"I should have offered him dinner," Greer said.

"He's tired. Tomorrow is another day for you to drive him crazy."

She looked at me, shocked. "I drive him crazy?"

"Just a little," I replied.

***

"This hasn't been a very good weekend for you," I said into the dark.

"It's been a great weekend. We were together," Lockie said, and felt for my hand under the sheet.

"You judged the show, I think that was too much standing, and then Nicole took a runner."

"Talia, I enjoyed the show because we were together. Nicole leaving the farm doesn't make any difference at all."

"Released into the wild, she'll talk."

"I doubt if anyone who knows me will believe her. I'm a better rider than she is. I had a more impressive junior career than she did since I was riding in the adult jumper division when I was fifteen. She's a petulant child with a bad attitude. Everyone knows that."

I held onto his hand tighter. "I don't want her to hurt you. You push yourself so hard and I know how difficult it must be at times. I don't want her flippant cruelty to take anything away from all you've achieved."

"Pack in there, Silly," he said.

I moved over until we were touching.

"You're on my side."

"Of course."

"It wasn't a question it was a statement. This is the question. Why would I need anything else?"

I held him until he fell asleep and then I held him until I fell asleep.

8

"BESIDES BEING CRAZY, she a liar," Betsey Harrowgate said. "I suppose it's the same thing, you can't have one without the other."

"What's she lying about?" I asked as we walked down the aisle so Betsey could see the horses.

"Nova Reeve isn't her real name. It's Tina. We caught her at it. When she entered college, she was Tina. Wrote for the newspaper and had her photo on the website. Then she had her consciousness raised, and became—"

"Nova," Greer supplied.

"Yup. Then she started hanging around us. There were just six of my side-saddle riders then. At first, she seemed interested, then she became a wretched screeching sister of the traveling lecture circuit. We tried to be polite but the tedious haranguing became too much."

"What did you do to get rid of her?"

"It was one of our finer moments, possibly. Since we thought everything she said was B.S., one of us left her a big, fresh present in her car while she was lecturing us on how to live our lives."

"Very proactive," I said.

"She never came back."

"Now she's found me," Greer said.

"Just tell us where she's going to be and we'll take care of her again."

We paused at the front door, and could see the horses spending their morning at pasture before the flies became intolerable. As I finished looking through the photo album, Betsey brought us, I laughed at the thought of this group of lady-like side-saddle riders, decorating Nova's passenger seat with a cow pie.

"We'll be at the Miry Brook Show. Of course, we'll alert everyone on social media. We have quite a large circle in the area," Betsey assured us.

"How many people?" I asked.

"Probably a hundred ladies in eight states. Some are too far away to attend, and it is the weekend of a huge festival for Victorian reenactors in Maryland. We like to stay active."

I handed her the album. "Thank you for offering to do a demonstration of the side-saddle apron. I'm sure it will be interesting for the children."

"We like to educate anyone who will listen. History didn't begin in this century." Betsey smiled.

"And it didn't end in the past, either," Greer replied.

Betsey perked up. "I like that."

"You might not if it was your family life. My sister's ancestors have been lost to time. My family can be traced back to the Norman Conquest."

"You're living history."

"No more than you, I just know the names, dates and all the sins they visited on us."

"Anyone famous?" Betsey asked, heading for her truck.

"They were all a bunch of crazy buggers," Greer replied.

She opened the door and got in. "My favorite kind! See you at Miry Brook. I'll have the article up on the website by tomorrow morning."

We waved goodbye and she drove away.

"So you're the only sane person in your family?" I asked.

"You have to ask? You've met my mother." Greer turned to walk into the barn.

"And don't look now."

I could see Victoria's expensive car come down the drive and park by the house.

"I have to leave anyway."

I grabbed her hand before she could get to her truck. "No, you don't. I'll be there. If she gets to be too much, we'll go to Eat Dog Eat and pick up some treats for Joly."

"That way we can see what Sassy has developed for the show."

"Right."

"I don't want to see Fifi."

"It's not noon yet. What makes you think she's awake?"

That got a smile out of Greer, and I opened the kitchen door.

"Lunch is almost ready. Do you want to eat inside or out?"

"It's a beautiful day and not hot yet. Out," I said.

Greer went to the sink and washed her hands. "I'll set the table. How many will there be? Three?"

"I've invited your mother," Jules said as Victoria entered the kitchen.

"Four," Greer replied, ignoring her mother's arrival. "Where's Fluffy?"

"She took a flight to London this morning. Divorce papers are being served," Victoria explained.

"Get out of town before the vampire bats descend. She has a real talent for creating chaos and then slipping away." Greer retrieved the Italian plates with the lemon decoration, then picked up the green and yellow napkins.

"And then she's going to Rowe House," Victoria said, casually.

80

The plates clattered onto the counter.

"Why."

"She needs a place to stay."

"Claridge's is booked solid?"

"They will find her in London. The wife is talking."

"Material for your new book?" Greer asked.

"I don't need to get ideas from Fifi," Victoria replied.

"Is she going to stay in my bedroom?"

Victoria regarded her with a look of surprise. "Your bedroom? You haven't been home for many years."

"This is my home," Greer said.

"Yes. I'm sure my parents consider your former bedroom a sanctuary and Fifi can choose one of the many others. The Garden Room, perhaps."

"It overlooks the walled garden, and has amazing needlework in floral designs, done when my ancestors weren't permitted to leave the house unattended and had lifetimes to kill," Greer said sharply.

"I assure you, they left the house. The women in the family have never been introverts."

Greer walked onto the terrace without replying.

"Fifi was quite good company," Victoria told Jules. "I can understand why men like her as much as they do."

"Why is that?" I asked.

"She's like a vacation. She's not serious. A man will have a good time, and then resume his normal life."

"What does that do for Fifi?" I wondered.

"She wants to be on holiday, too."

"Her whole life has been a vacation," Jules said. "She barely made it through school, then my father got her a job in the business. She lasted a month. She got another job, lasted two weeks. The last job she didn't bother going to the office once."

"She's very beautiful with the dark hair and light blue eyes. I'm sure she'll make a wealthy man fine arm candy."

"What a goal to have," Greer replied, coming back into the kitchen.

"She just broke up someone's marriage," I said. "What's wrong with him?"

Victoria paused for a moment. "He doesn't play for her team."

"Excuse me?"

"He prefers men," Victoria said.

"He's a famous movie star."

Jules patted me on the shoulder as she went to the terrace. "Yes, and now everyone is quite sure he likes women. This publicity will last until his next movie release."

I looked at Greer. "Am I the only one who didn't know?"

"You don't even go to the movies. How would you know?"

"That's true. I lead a very sheltered life where pop culture is concerned."

"We don't need it," Greer said, leaving the house with Joly following at her feet.

"Why would Fifi date him then? What was in it for her?" I asked.

They looked at me.

"What?"

"Money and other valuable considerations. Women like that get a credit card, they shop on Rodeo Drive, they pick up some trinkets at Lucarno's Luxury Jeweler, they go to the Jaguar dealership for a little runabout. It's worth it to the actor and the studio. The more the girlfriend spends, the more likely it will make the entertainment news and leave no doubts in anyone's mind that he does like girls."

"Why not just tell the truth?"

"You're going to have a male action star and sex symbol say he's just acting?"

"He is acting to start with. How is this such a stretch?"

"It's a fantasy," Victoria said. "Part of the illusion entertainment creates is to make the audience think they could be a character in the story. This very handsome man or beautiful woman could want them. They could be sexy, desirable, strong, agile, brave—"

"And good in bed," Greer added.

Victoria nodded. "That façade, that white lie, must be preserved. People are happy to be lied to in that way. They read the book or see a movie and come away satisfied. They don't want the truth. They have the truth in their real lives.

Going to the movies is less expensive than going away for the weekend."

"And probably be disappointed because it rains the entire time," Jules said.

"Don't worry if you don't get it, you're better off not getting it," Greer told me as she sat at the table.

I looked at Jules.

"I don't get it and it's been explained to me. I was happy to leave Los Angeles. Eat your lunch. And let's change the subject. Fifi is three thousand miles away—"

"In my bedroom!" Greer said.

Victoria squeezed a slice of fresh lemon into her tea. "Call your grandmother and tell her that the Red Rose Room is off limits. I assure you, she knows that, but don't take my word for it."

Greer took her phone out and keyed in a number.

Jules and I concentrated on our grilled chicken salads.

"Hi, Grandmother. Yes, I've missed you, too. We're very busy here, I'll visit...sometime." There was a pause. "I'm glad my mother has reported back all the news." Greer shot Victoria a look. "I believe you're having a houseguest. Yes, she's lovely, and inflicted herself on us, too."

"No, that's fine," Jules said to me. "I feel the same way about Fifi most of the time."

Victoria shrugged.

"You only had her for a few days. If you have to put up with the shenanigans for years, the adventure of it wears thin."

My phone began ringing. Lockie. I clicked it on. "Hi."

"We're just turning onto the road to the farm. Meet us at the barn. We have a present for Greer. Don't spoil the surprise."

"Okay. See you. Bye." I clicked off.

Greer was just finishing her conversation with her grandmother.

"That was Lockie and he wants us to meet them at the barn."

"I didn't eat lunch," Greer protested.

"We'll all eat together." I stood.

Cam's truck and trailer came slowly down the driveway. It was easy to tell if there was an occupant because of the speed and the sound the trailer made empty or carrying a horse.

Greer pushed away from the table and started walking toward the barn with me. "Who's in the trailer?"

"I have no idea. When Lockie left, he said they were going to see a man about a horse. That can mean anything."

"Maybe Cam will lease Obi."

"I think Obi will stay here. Now that there's real money in hunter derbies, as proven by his ability to buy Obi after a weekend, Cam can do those."

"I thought he wanted to do Grand Prix," Greer said. "That's what they were training Teche's horses for, wasn't it?"

"Yes. I don't know what Cam's plans are. Retiring Whiskey changed his future."

"He still has Jetzt."

"Who's not ready to do anything but canter around and be introduced to what will be asked of him."

"He's got Counterpoint."

Cam was the better rider for him. Greer was perfect on Tea and even Bria, but I wouldn't say that to her. She was good on Counterpoint and she could have kept him at an amateur level. I didn't think her heart was into the bigger fences and bigger competitions. Maybe in another year or two, she'd be ready. Right now, Greer felt comfortable with side-saddle and the hunter divisions. There was no need to do anything she didn't want to do. Those days were behind us.

We stopped to watch Cam back a dark bay colt off the trailer.

"Two year old?" I asked.

"Good eye, Tal," Lockie said.

Cam held out the lead to Greer. "He's for you."

"He's for me in what way?"

Cam took her hand and pushed the rope into it. "He's yours. His name is Partial Stranger. You can raise him, train him, let him sit in the field for the rest of his life. It's up to you."

The colt frisked her pocket for the carrots she carried, so Greer offered him a piece.

"Now you're friends," Cam said. "What's for lunch?" He and Lockie headed for the house.

Cap came out of the barn and started up the drive. "Nice horse," she commented as she walked by.

That was an understatement. This was a beautiful colt, with a white strip down his face and a coat so shiny you could nearly use it for a mirror.

"What am I supposed to do with this horse?"

"Put him in the lower barn with Lockie's trainees."

"His name isn't Partial Stranger," Greer insisted.

"Why not?"

"Cam and I had a discussion and I called him a complete stranger and he said he was a partial stranger. I can see you pressing your lips together so you won't laugh."

"Come on, Greer, admit it. Cam is smart and funny."

"And your point is?"

We walked to the lower barn with the colt's nose on her pocket.

"You're lucky. Nicole was interested in him but his interests are elsewhere. Enjoy him. Life is short."

The stall next to Tsai's was empty so we opened the door.

"What if—"

"No. There are always unknowns in life. Control the things you can and don't worry about the rest." I grabbed a couple flakes of hay from the cart.

"Isn't that how I screwed my life up before?"

I tossed the hay to the colt. "Were you controlling anything before?"

Greer thought for a moment. "No."

"Like anything, go slow. Your first lesson with Bertie Warner wasn't over fences, was it?"

"No." She removed his leg wraps and bell boots.

"You don't rush. You get confirmed at one level before you move on to the next."

"That's true."

I closed the colt's stall door. "If you like him, give Cam a chance."

Greer leaned against the door and the colt came over to us. She put her hand on his nose and there was a long pause. "Nothing bad has ever happened to him."

"Probably not, and now you're in control of his entire life."

"Some horses live through a nightmare," Greer said.

"I think so, but not here."

"I want him to have a perfect life."

No one has a perfect life but I didn't want to say that to her. "I think we use horses to repair our own lives. If we can make their lives trouble-free then it doesn't matter so much if ours are a mess."

"Do you believe that?"

"Yes. We think we can redeem ourselves through them."

"Can we?"

I shrugged. "I don't know, but it's worth a try."

Greer gave the colt another piece of carrot that he took from her palm enthusiastically.

We walked up to the house and found only our seats left open at the table on the terrace. My father had returned from the trip he had been on and was at the head. Lockie was at the foot. It was exactly how everything should be and I didn't even object to Victoria sitting between my father and Cam.

Greer stopped and looked at her mother sitting there comfortably.

"Come here, Gracie, I saved your seat," Cam said.

I sat at my place between Lockie and Jules. "Where did you get the colt?"

"He was bred by a woman I know in Massachusetts," Cam replied. "She needed to find him a good home so we got him at a fire sale price."

"What's his real name?" Greer asked.

"It's whatever you want it to be," Cam told her.

"What's his breed?"

"American Warmblood."

"Then he has years before he does anything."

Lockie nodded. "Warmbloods are usually started later because they mature later."

"Unless someone sees dollar signs instead of the horse," Greer replied.

"True," Lockie admitted. "I don't like to see a young horse hurried and now you have one who is a clean slate. Take your time."

I thought about CB, and what he must have gone through in order to make him as quirky as he was. It was a fortunate horse who wound up with a good trainer concerned about his well-being.

"Things were different when I was a girl," Victoria began.

"During the reign of Elizabeth Regina?" Greer asked.

Victoria laughed. "You have a very droll sense of humor, darling. A good horse was one who would carry you safely across-country. I never understood what Princess Anne was on about with the competition and the Olympics."

"But you rode Dice at that event last month," Lockie said.

"When you have someone in the family as proficient as Greer, it's hard for it to go unnoticed."

I tried kicking Greer's foot under the table to warn her not to say anything.

"That's my foot," Cam said to me.

"I thought I'd have a go at it. He's a perfectly nice horse and Greg's a good coach. I have plenty of free time."

"Not writing?" Jules asked.

"Maybe Aria and—"

"Gilbert," Greer supplied.

"Gillette," Victoria said, "will be married to predictable results."

Jules looked up. "What would those be?"

"She's the loose tart, so she'll cheat on him while he's riding the Grand Prix circuit," Cap replied.

"The story writes itself," Jules said.

"That would be delightful, but unfortunately I have to be there at least part of the time." Victoria finished her iced tea. "I remember when we didn't have iced drinks in England. Now it's expected."

"My, my, how times do change."

"Speaking of time, Greer, I thought you would be interested to know that a television series is going to be shot at Rowe House."

Greer stared at her mother. "Which Rowe House."

"The one with your bedroom."

"A travel documentary?"

"No. This is one of those history dramas so popular now. It's about Rosamund Hasart."

"Why would anyone make a movie about her?" Greer said sharply.

"What about her," I asked.

"During the War of the Roses, she was a spy or, better put, an opportunist. Double dealing her way to a fortune in land and jewels. Playing both sides, the Lancastrians and the Yorkists. She was typical of our family, completely bereft of any morality."

Victoria gently wiped her lips with her napkin.

"Why would you agree to this?"

"I had nothing to do with it. Rowe House belongs to your grandfather and he needs the money."

"You have money."

"I have a small nest egg but I don't have the kind of money needed to buy Rowe House."

"Upkeep, then."

"You haven't been there in years. What's suddenly so important about that house?"

"It's the family house!"

"The bereft of all morality family that you have renounced at every turn."

"Then sell it to a rock star who can afford it! Of course they'll have go-carts races in the Great Hall."

"The Cavaliers rode horses through there so why not. You're ignoring the fact that it's not mine to sell. Your grandfather signed the contract to have the movie filmed on-site."

"He's *non compis mentos*!"

"It's a done deal and filming starts at the beginning of the month. The gardens are being completely replanted. Rowe House will look more beautiful than it has in centuries."

"This must be stopped," Greer exclaimed, pushing her chair back so quickly that Joly had to scoot out of the way.

"You have your life here, it doesn't make any difference what they do over there," I said.

"If someone was going to film a cheesy movie here, you'd protest," Greer countered.

Lockie looked at me.

I thought for a moment. "Yes, I would."

"Then come with me to England. We'll take the first flight we can get."

"You have the Miry Brook show," Jules said.

"I don't want to be there more than a few days," Greer replied.

"Tal. We have horses in training," Lockie said. "You have the pony riders."

"We'll be back by the weekend, right, Greer? Buck, Cap and Freddi will be able to handle the schedule. Give CB a couple days off. It doesn't make any difference to him. It's not as though Miry Brook will be any more difficult than what he does most days."

"You're forgetting something else," Victoria said. "Fifi will be there."

Greer grimaced.

"We'll avoid her," I said.

"Is the house that large," Jules asked.

"She'll be asleep most of the time," I replied.

"I'll book the flight. Go pack." Greer defaulted into her organize everything mode and went into the house with her phone against her ear.

There was silence at the table.

"It's only for a few days," Jules reminded everyone.

***

"It's only for a few days," I told Lockie later that evening.

"In June!" he replied. "I need you here. This is bad timing, Tal."

"Greer needs me."

"I need you." He was angry and strode into the kitchen.

"Have Cam stay here at the carriage house with you."

"What's a few days?" he shouted.

"A couple, two, three, four. We'll be back before the weekend."

Lockie appeared with a glass of water and his evening meds. "Before or by?"

I raised my hands. "I don't know what the distinction is."

"Anytime you go somewhere, it winds up being a longer trip than planned." He swallowed the pills.

"Would you prefer it if I didn't go?"

"Of course I would prefer that."

I waited for him to complete the thought.

"I'm not suggesting you stay home and leave Greer to her own devices. That doesn't mean I like the trip or believe it will achieve what she says she wants. She's not going to prevent a movie being made at the old homestead."

"She feels as though she must do something," I said. "It's futile but Greer takes on causes. This time she can't help but think of all the times she does succeed. The important part is to try."

"I understand the sentiment. No one bats a thousand but tilting at windmills is a waste of time."

"Lockie. She needs to do this. It's not about stopping the production. It's about going back to the vipers' nest."

He laughed. "I'm sorry. I sincerely doubt if they're vipers. By the sound of her grandparents, they're clinically self-centered but hardly vicious."

"They didn't treat her very well."

"Most of us have not been treated very well. That's part of the growing up process. You learn from it and become an adult. If you don't learn from it, you're forever a child."

"I was treated well. Did I grow up yet? Am I consigned to forever be a child?"

Lockie reached out and gently stroked my hair the way I'd seen him do to a horse that needed reassurance. "I didn't say that was the only way to gain maturity. You know how to love. That's one reason why I don't want you to go. Cam might stay here as your long-distance babysitter, but he can't take your place."

I put my hand on his. "I'm not choosing Greer instead of you."

"You're triaging us."

"What?"

"You're staying with the person who needs you most right now."

"Right now, I'm with the person I need most."

"Silly. You're turning into quite the sweet-talker. Just for that, we'll watch the salsa showdown show."

We started up the stairs.

"There is no such thing."

"Are you sure? I could have sworn I saw something that stultifyingly boring."

$\backsim$ 9 $\backsim$

WITH VICTORIA FOOTING THE BILL for the tickets, or courtesy of *Tight Chaps and Loose Tarts* as she said, we arrived at London's Heathrow Airport and picked up the car she rented for us. Off we went to our destiny with Greer's ancestor, spy/mistress/party girl Rosamund Hasart.

I had never been to England before and it was almost impossible to get any indication of what it looked like, Greer was driving so fast and so grimly. We drove for several hours on a highway, took an exit ramp and started going through the countryside where she had to slow down. The road was wide enough for a hay wagon, not two cars going in opposite directions.

By the time I was feeling that I had traveled enough for one day, we reached the town of Little Swerden and it was iconically British. The streets were narrow, the houses were older than any in Newbury by at least three hundred years, and, but for the modern cars and satellite dishes, we could have been time travelers.

It was starting to drizzle and Greer turned on the windshield wipers. "Welcome to England," she said sourly. "Yesterday was the last you've seen of the sun until we get back to the farm."

"This is so cute."

"Uh huh. There's a Sainsbury outside of town."

"What's that?"

"Supermarket, so not cute."

We reached the ancestral home, deep in the countryside, with a sign on an old stone pillar that said Rowe House, and had to wait for a small tour bus to leave the driveway before we could enter.

The driveway was longer than the one at the farm. "Does all this belong to your family?"

"A thousand acres is all that's left. We used to own the whole town, but that was a very long time ago. Don't expect a castle. It's just a house."

"The definition is slightly different though, right?"

There was an old stone bridge ahead and water.

"A moat?" I asked.

"It's river. Some running water. It's barely more than what's in our stream."

"We don't have a bridge over the stream."

"Tch."

The house became visible, a huge gray stone, three story building, with narrow chimneys everywhere and what looked like a slate roof covered with moss. The windows were small paned and set with iron. Glass had been expensive and difficult to obtain in the large sizes, that we were accustomed to now, when this house had been built.

There were climbing red roses competing with the ivy and purple flowers up the outside walls. The beds were an untamed riot of growth, greens, and blooms with no organization whatsoever. It was fantastic.

"I can't bear this," Greer said. "There shouldn't be tourists dragging the shopping bags wearing their plastic shoes and baggy clothes from the ASDA clearance bin."

"What's ASDA?"

"Discount store."

"Maybe they can't afford designer outfits," I replied.

"Put your good clothes on when you go out. Don't look like a slob."

Ninety percent of the passengers on the jet had been wearing comfortable clothes. Greer traveled in style. I felt as if I had gone over Niagara Falls in a wheelbarrow and she looked as if she had just been the model for a fashion magazine photo shoot.

"People behave up to or down to their clothing," she said.

"I'll try to remember that."

"Look at all these cars leaving their oil drippings on my white pebbles. It's disgusting."

I didn't see oil drippings but there were tourists strolling around the grounds wearing shorts when they definitely should have chosen something else.

After parking, we got out and Greer marched us up to the front door.

There was a ticket-taker preventing our entering. "Can't let you through without a ticket. They have to be purchased in advance. Come back tomorrow."

"Are you daft? This is my home. I'm Lady Greer Rowe." She pushed past him and I followed.

"I'm with her," I said to the man, hurrying along.

"Oh, will you look at this? Plastic floor runners!"

The only time I had been in a building similar to this was when my mother and I had spent a weekend in Newport, Rhode Island. This building was larger than the public library in Newbury.

Greer tried to go through a door, but it was locked. The next one she tried was also locked. I hoped she would not take her mounting frustration out on it.

"What tour are you supposed to be on?" A female guide said to us as she came by with a merry band of lookie-loos. "Those doors go to the private residence."

"That's the point."

"If you don't leave, I shall call the security guard."

"By all means, do," Greer replied. "Anything, as long as I get into the house."

"They only place you'll go is the constabulary."

This was wonderful. Being arrested for going home. Lockie wasn't going to believe me when I told him.

"Call your grandmother," I suggested.

"I have to call my grandmother from the dog room?"

"This is the dog room?"

"In years gone by, it was."

A wood-paneled room for themselves, with oil paintings of their previous masters. Even the dogs lived better than most people in that time.

"Is this the room the Cavaliers rode through?"

Phone to her ear, Greer looked at me in surprise. "That was the Great Hall."

I turned slowly around the enormous room. A horse could fit in here.

"Grandmother, I'm in the dog room and the door's locked." She paused. "Some person from the village is threatening to have me arrested for trespassing." Greer glared at the docent.

This was not going to be an easy few days.

A couple minutes later, with warning expressions exchanged, the door opened and another Lady Rowe appeared.

"Greer, darling. It's so good to see you."

The sleek woman who looked like a slightly older version of Victoria air-kissed her granddaughter.

She stepped back and glanced toward me. "And this must be your father's other daughter."

"My sister's name is Talia," Greer replied firmly.

"I'm sure it is. It's such a bother to remember everything like an encyclopedia."

I had the momentary urge to grab Greer's hand, run out of there, jump in the car and head back to the airport but I squelched it and followed them further into the house.

"Did you bring any luggage? I suppose you have. Raymond will bring it from the car. How long will you be with us?"

"Until Friday morning."

"That will be lovely, I'm sure. And why are you visiting us?"

"To make Grandfather see reason about renting the house out to the film production company."

"The contract is signed and they'll be pottering about before you leave. Did you know we have another guest? A lovely woman. Fifi Finzi. Such a delightful girl."

Lady Rowe bought us into a large wood-paneled room with an oak-beamed vaulted ceiling. Paintings and antlers hung on the walls as well as armor, shields, helmets, and swords. A fireplace many times the size of ours at the farm was along the inside wall.

It wasn't difficult to know where Victoria picked up her decorating sense, as Lockie's carriage house had the same feel with the dark red tones, leather furniture, equestrian oils, and ivory accents.

There was no one in the room except us.

"Your grandfather will be along presently. Would you like some tea?"

Yes, please," I said.

There was a pause that made me feel I wasn't the one being asked but that was probably just my imagination.

Lady Rowe left by another door.

"Is it okay if I sit down?"

"You don't need special dispensation to sit," Greer replied and went to the windows that reached to the ceiling.

On the mantel, a clock ticked loudly.

"It's a beautiful house," I said, "from what I've seen so far."

"Not home."

"No, not to me. It's more like a museum, but if this is what you're accustomed to, I'm sure it...is..." I was at a loss for words.

Anything I said could be taken as an insult and that wasn't what I intended. Rowe House was fantastic, fairy tale, like something I had seen in movies. It was no wonder a production company wanted to shoot here. No set building was required, everything was already in place, all they needed was costumes and actors. Perhaps the clothing was in the attic. If this house had an attic.

"It's cold, old, and poorly heated," Greer said. "It's altogether uncomfortable but the British like this kind of thing."

"And you are?"

"Being English is a fact of my birth. Maybe we shouldn't have made this trip."

"It was important to you."

Greer turned to me. "Why?"

"It's a connection with your family that you can trace back over a thousand years. I wish I could do that."

"We'll do that. We'll find the records."

I shrugged. "Records were destroyed over the centuries. It wasn't the same as for the Rowes."

"Being royalty means being breeding stock."

I laughed. "You're the best sister. You really do know how to make a bad situation better."

She shook her head.

"We can leave at any time."

"I need to talk to my grandfather."

"I understand."

"We have to go to the tea, it's not coming to us," Greer said and looped her arm through mine.

"I'm a serf. I don't know the royal rules."

"Eating through the house isn't done."

"I'll make a note of that."

Greer maneuvered me through rooms and passageways until we reached a small, for Rowe House, room overlooking the garden. It was raining, the windows were covered with ivy and assorted greenery, and the illumination was what one might expect in the late fourteen hundreds. Hard to see your hand in front of your face.

Tea at the farm meant Jules had made small tarts, petit fours, or buttery cookies. There would be several pots of tea because we each had a favorite. This was the home of minor royalty, so I assumed it had to be far more sophisticated. What we found on the table was a pot of hot water, some tea bags, and a plate of packaged cookies.

"Thank you, Lady Rowe. I hope you didn't go to too much trouble for us," I said, then wondered if I was permitted to speak first or did I have to wait for the king to address me.

"It was no trouble," she replied.

"Where's Grandfather?" Greer asked.

"He went with Simon to check on the herd of cows."

"They raise beef," Greer said to me.

I fiddled with the tea bag, not knowing where to put it after extracting it from my cup. "Really? It must be delicious with all that green grass as forage."

"It's highly prized in Upper Swerden's Michelin three-star restaurant," Lady Rowe said. "It's received excellent reviews. We're thinking about having a shop in the barn and selling the beef there, along with the Rowe House honey. There is local cheese which would be a good item, too."

"A shop?" Greer was stunned. "Tourists and a shop?"

"Yes, and film production. That's what people like us do these days. Your mother doesn't seem to want to help out."

I sipped my tea but it was cold already.

"This house has existed for hundreds of years and it was able to support itself," Greer said.

"That's when one didn't pay the serfs, they paid us," Lady Rowe replied.

"Maybe Grandfather shouldn't have spent all that time in Monte Carlo playing Chemin de Fer."

"Everyone needs a mini-break."

"From what? What has he ever done?"

"May I remind you that your Grandfather worked in the City?"

"When was that?"

"What city?" I whispered.

"The financial district of London," Greer replied.

Lady Rowe stood. "Dinner will be at eight. Please dress, we have company."

"We're company," Greer replied.

Her grandmother looked at us. "Hardly." She left the room.

"Are we supposed to take the dishes to the kitchen?"

Greer pushed away from the table. "There's a woman from Little Swerden who takes care of the kitchen chores for them. Don't get excited. She's nothing like Jules."

I followed Greer through the hallway and up a staircase. "So Fifi is company but we're not."

"You seem to have analyzed the situation correctly." Greer stopped at a door. "This is my room."

"Where am I staying, the dog room?"

Greer pointed to my suitcase positioned down the hall. "The Seal Room."

We were nowhere near the ocean. Were there fresh water seals? "What kind of seals? Like otters?"

"Not animals, wax. There is a display of all the seals the family has used since the Middle Ages. At least, the ones that survived. If that collection was sold, it would be worth—" Greer sighed.

"Is it better to sell honey out of a shop than to sell the stamps?"

"I don't know."

Greer looked exhausted.

"Why don't you lie down for a while? I'll call home and make sure they're surviving without us."

"We flew three thousand miles and my grandfather couldn't leave the herd long enough to greet us."

"Maybe he's checking for hoof-rot," I suggested.

"He wouldn't know it if he saw it." Greer went into her bedroom and closed the door.

I brought my suitcase into the bedroom and looked around. The walls were a dark red fabric, the ceiling had dark oak beams and a chandelier with candle-style lights. The bed was an enormous oak four-poster, with draperies, swags, and decorative pillows. There were portrait and landscape paintings in gilt frames. Swords were crossed over the fireplace. There was a fire because it was needed. The room was cold and damp.

Walking around in disbelief, I reminded myself that almost everything in the room was older than the town I lived in, then paused at the window. Through the rain, the river with a small bridge made of stones could be seen below and then lush green fields undulated to the horizon.

Turning away, I reached into my bag for my phone and hoped there was service here. Lockie's phone rang, then he picked up.

"Hi."

"Hi."

"What's wrong?"

"This explains so much."

"That's probably why she wanted you to come along, so you could see for yourself."

"It's a fantastic country home. You wouldn't believe the grandeur of my bedroom. It's June. There are fires in most of the fireplaces. The building is stone. It's raining and cold yet warmer than the grandmother. The grandfather didn't bother to or didn't remember to show up to welcome Greer for her visit."

"The trip was designed to be a confrontation, so maybe the old sod wants to avoid it and her."

I sat on the bed. "What kind of people are these?"

"Upper class. Better than the likes of us."

"Please have Cam call her."

"No, I will not. That's between them," he replied.

There was no point in pressing Lockie on this. "Are you taking the Zuckerlumpens today or is Cap?"

"I am."

"Did you ride CB?"

"Yes, I did this morning. He objects to me. He complies with my requests but only just so far. Put it this way, he's not a *freudigen geist* with me."

CB's papered name translated into English meant Joyful Spirit. I didn't know how to convince the two of them to play nice. It felt as though CB didn't see why he should cooperate fully with Lockie when he had been mistreated earlier in life. He was rebelling in the only way he knew how by doing what was asked but doing it without enthusiasm, without the brilliance he was so capable of.

I was not the rider to get the best performance from CB and he knew it. He was my pet pony, my babysitter. Lockie, with his higher standards and greater experience, had expectations. CB was unwilling to meet those standards.

Perhaps it was time to give up and I had wrestled with that question many times over the past months. I kept thinking that was the wrong lesson for both of them to learn.

Lockie needed to be less demanding technically, and CB needed to learn how to fully express his talents. They needed to become friends. I thought the beer drinking together would bridge the gap between them, and CB certainly appreciated a good brew but that was on the ground. They needed to be friends at work but I wasn't clever enough to know how to arrange this. I suspected that if Lockie's dressage master, Mauritz Schencker, was asked, the answer would be more training. Since CB had had a surfeit of training, I suspected that plan would backfire.

"Ride him bareback," I said. "Get Cam, Cap and Buck to play tag with you."

"Talia, are you serious?"

"Yes." I thought for a moment. "Do you remember when you first started riding, how much fun you had? What would you have done if someone had given you a horse then, before you started to show?"

"Am I supposed to answer?" Lockie asked.

"Yes. Cam used to go on camp-outs with Remington. They went everywhere, they explored, got lost, got found."

"You want me to camp out with an upper level dressage horse?"

"He's a failed upper level dressage horse. Right now, he's my pet pony. Take CB to the state park and sleep with him."

"What if he's hurt?"

"Accidents happen even if you're careful. Cam and Remi survived it, so will you two."

There was silence on the other end. "Aly Beck just arrived with the girls, so I have to go. Are you going to call me later?"

"Of course. Dinner should be brilliant here. At least we might have home-raised beef. The rest of it is going to be sour sops."

"When are you coming home?" Lockie asked.

"You didn't get the horses ridden yet?"

"Last night I watched an hour of extreme martial arts and no one was there to complain."

"I said to have Cam stay with you."

"He was watching with me."

I laughed.

"It wasn't the same."

"Friday sometime, I promise, even if I have to leave Greer here."

"Talk to you later, Silly."

"Bye, Lockie."

I clicked off and didn't get up from the bed, wondering if I could leave Greer here alone with her grandparents and Fifi. No. She'd have to come home with me. Whatever she was trying to accomplish, she had to hurry up and do it so we could get back to our real home.

There was a tap at my door. "Tal."

"Come on in."

Greer entered. "This looks like a medieval bordello. Is the mattress as bad as ever?" She sat next to me. "Yes. It's probably the original Tudor mattress made of horsehair."

"Yours is...?"

"Modern. When we moved here from France, my mother bought us both new mattresses and sheets so we weren't sleeping on threadbare linens that we could put our feet through in the middle of the night."

"I heard about this historic house and the title. We were living in a small apartment and lucky when the sun shone through one of the windows. I imagined you were living like a princess in a castle."

"Never. School was worse than this. Why didn't Dad get you a nicer place to live?"

"Because my mother had dignity if nothing else. We did move once she was diagnosed. Someplace more convenient and comfortable."

"My mother has a title but no dignity."

"People are capable of changing. Sometimes it sneaks up on you without even realizing it. Then one day you think things aren't the way they had been."

"That's a very positive way of looking at life, but don't expect my mother to turn into someone you want to have dinner with."

I smiled.

"Speaking of dinner, don't change if you don't want to. This is a country house not Buckingham Palace."

"When you lived here—"

"—Ick."

"Did you pretend that you were living in the past, the Elizabethan era?"

"Or during the War of the Roses? Thanks to Grandfather they'll be play acting all through the house."

"No?"

"Definitely not. I had no one to play with. Sometimes Harriett de Bellem would drop off her daughter, Iona, for an afternoon of appropriate activities."

"You must have wanted to tear your hair out."

"Her hair. I always quite liked my hair."

"You haven't been going to the hairdresser like you used to."

"It's not only that I don't have time, it seems..."

I waited for her to find the word she wanted without prompting.

"Small. Trish manages to get to the hospital wards and senior centers with Oliver for the Ambassador of Cheer events not needing new outfits or hairstyles."

"Don't compare yourself to her. You're running a charity. If you don't look professional, people will think you handle your work with the same careless attitude you present yourself."

"Then they won't give me their money."

"Exactly," I replied. "Are they giving you their money?"

"Amanda keeps a close eye on the books and you know how hard it is to get any kind of compliment but she hasn't complained either." Greer lay back on the bed. "Every bit as uncomfortable as ever. Nothing will ever be perfect, will it?"

"No. We try to perfect what's around us but we'll always fail," I replied.

"Isn't that a rather gloomy worldview?"

"I don't think so. You try. Sometimes you succeed. Sometimes you fail. That's normal. You reorganize and keep going with more experience."

"Coming from this family prepared me for a life that ceased to exist four hundred years ago."

I laughed.

"I'm going to fail now, right?"

"I think so," I replied.

"Believing that, why did you make the trip with me?"

"I thought you needed the company. Besides, I've never stayed in an English country house." I gestured at the canopy over the bed, and the sabers hanging on the wall. "I was never so grand as this."

"Remember that poem about returning to where you started and knowing the place for the first time?"

"Yes."

"I'm seeing Rowe House with new eyes."

"Let's call Jules." I picked up my cell phone. "You can eavesdrop as I tell her how your grandmother's attitude was like she thought it would be so nice if I wasn't here."

Greer smiled. "She feels the same about me."

I pressed speed dial for the house. "I talked to Lockie a while ago and he wants us to come back promptly."

"Fine by me."

"You're not going to stick it out until your change your grandfather's mind?"

"No. I'm going to say what I think about using the house for something as grubby as a movie about Rosamund, and he's going to do what he wants to do regardless. I'm sure she'll be portrayed as a right little tart."

"You mean sexy her up for ratings?"

"She was a right little tart, so that would be accurate."

Jules picked up the phone in Connecticut.

"Hi, Jules. Remember me?"

***

At eight, we went downstairs for dinner. It seemed to be in progress and there were a few people with before dinner drinks in their hands. Fifi was, as might be expected, in the center of the small crowd and they were flirting madly with her.

"This is going to be an endless meal," Greer said as we entered the dining hall, a long rather narrow room with red draped windows overlooking the river. There was a large chandelier, wall-sconces with lit candles, candles on the table and a fire in the fireplace. It was still so dark it was difficult to find the seats.

Greer took my hand and guided me to a place beside hers and we sat.

Fifi and the gentlemen bantered, while Lady Rowe organized the service of the meal. Then Lord Rowe entered and Greer had been correct in assuming he would be dressed for a good hike through the briars.

"Greer and your relative. How nice for you to join us."

"Thank you for welcoming me into your lovely home," I replied, guessing I was not supposed to speak.

"Yes," Lady Rowe replied, not looking at me.

I leaned over to Greer. "I didn't unpack. We can drive back to London tonight, and I'll bring you home where you are loved and we'll protect you."

"Stick it out with me," she whispered back.

"Okay."

The first course was served. I didn't recognize any of the food on the table. There was a fluffy beige substance that I poked at. "What is it?"

"I have no idea. What century does this food represent?" Greer asked.

"Fifteenth," Lady Rowe replied. "That's parsnip mousse with ground almonds and claret."

I tried to groan softly.

"What's this?" Greer asked, pointing to a platter full of miniature brown torpedoes.

"Dates stuffed with eggs and cheese," Lady Rowe said. "They were a delicacy."

"Why aren't we having real food?"

Lord Rowe popped a date into his mouth. "Because we are preparing for the movie."

"Niall Fitzwarren," the man across from me said as he reached over to shake my hand. "I'm the producer of *The King's Courtesan*—"

"Trull would be more accurate," Greer said.

"When we make this series—"

"It's a series?"

"Yes, they all are," Lady Rowe informed us.

As though she had a lifetime of being in the film industry.

"—we're striving for accuracy. The costumes, the appurtenances, even the food will be historically accurate."

Greer yawned. "Excuse me. Jet lag."

"It sounds like great fun to me," Fifi chimed in. "But to the Sisters Grimm here..."

The words were so soft, I wasn't sure I heard her correctly until Greer nearly levitated off her chair in anger.

"If you have something to say about us, say it out loud not in a pansy passive-aggressive voice."

"You're not the girls-just-want-to-have-fun type, you'll admit to that fact, won't you?" Fifi asked. "The movie will be like one long costume party."

I touched Greer's leg under the table.

"How can you be Julcs's sister?" Greer was baffled.

"You don't know how many times I've wondered the same thing!" Fifi batted her eyelashes at Niall.

Lord Rowe laughed and took a big gulp from the goblet in front of his place.

It was beginning to feel reminiscent of the lunchroom at the Briar School with the in-crowd and the misbegottens.

The first course was swept away, and the entrée was served.

"What's this?" Greer asked looking at her plate.

"Wild boar," Lady Rowe replied.

Greer pushed it away from her, as did I.

"It's a great delicacy. I had it at Wolfgang Puck's restaurant." Fifi cut into the meat.

"Is the Tabard Inn still there?" Greer stood.

"It's been in the center of town since the late fourteen hundreds, I believe," Lady Rowe replied without looking up.

"We'll eat there. Come with me, Grimmula."

No one tried to talk her out of leaving, not that I expected she would have but it would have been the right thing to do.

We got into the rental car, zoomed off the estate and headed toward town.

"Misplaced loyalty," Greer finally said as we found a place to park in Little Swerden.

"You?"

She pulled open the door to the inn and waited for me to enter.

"Yes. I had a fantasy about being one of the oldest aristocratic families in England, going back to the Domesday Book. That tradition was supposed to mean something."

"It does."

"They're lunatics." She found an empty table and acquired it. "They don't care about the family or the house. They're frittering it all away."

"I'm not taking their side, but there will be income from this movie. Lots of houses in England are used in period dramas. Hepplewhite."

"What?"

"That's probably not the name of the estate. Stounsbury? I read about it somewhere. It was used in *Four Weddings and a Funeral* and...and..."

"*Austin Powers? Monty Python?*"

"No, some Thomas Hardy thing. It's a way to generate income."

"Other families manage to keep their homes private without renting them out like marquees."

"What?" I was definitely not following her.

"Rent-a-Tent. Or worse. It demeans the house by renting it out for weddings and business promotions."

"Greer—"

"Letting people pretend it's theirs for a few hours when they have no connection to the history. Drinking too much and puking in the Tudor Knot Garden. I can imagine what they'd do by the lake. 'Take me now or lose me forever'. I think that's on Rosamund's coat of arms."

"Put the revelry aside. To bring awareness and money for the Miry Brook Show, you made the video. How is that different?"

"You know it's different," Greer said.

I didn't, really.

The waitress came over. "What can I get for you?"

"Do you have roast beef?" Greer asked.

"From the herd at Rowe House. With Yorkshire pudding."

Greer threw me a look.

"Two."

"Brilliant." The waitress left.

"I don't even recognize these people."

"Have they changed so much since you lived here?"

"No," Greer said. "I have."

***

We returned to Rowe House and avoiding the dining hall, went straight to our rooms. I undressed, took a quick shower, then got into bed.

I wouldn't really want to pay to stay here overnight. The mattress was old and uncomfortable and the room seemed cold. But if staying in an English country house was your thing, this would ring all your bells.

That was undoubtedly the next step in the transformation of Rowe House. I didn't see Lady Rowe as a welcoming hostess, but perhaps she could turn on the charm for strangers in a way she didn't do for her granddaughter and relative.

The longer I was in the house, the less I understood why Greer wanted to make the trip. She had to know that once her grandparents had made the decision to throw open the house and family history to the film company, they would already be too far into the process to back out.

In a way, this was a good solution for them. I wasn't sure there was enough money to be had from this one movie, but if it kept the house in the family instead of going to the National Trust, then that was what was most important.

Lord Rowe was only a caretaker, not an owner. He was one individual in a thousand years of descendants, perhaps making a good decision, perhaps not. Victoria would inherit the estate and do better with it. Or maybe worse.

Maybe she didn't want it either. Victoria was making no effort to set up housekeeping in England. She had a picturesque New England farm that obviously she could afford and seemed to be enjoying her independence.

Rowe House wasn't even a money pit. It was a bottomless chasm. The upkeep had to be staggering. Fortunately, for Lord Rowe, his father had replaced the roof. If that had to be done now with it now being a Grade 1 listed house, requiring adherence to maintenance specifications, the cost would have made a rock star weak in the knees.

One thing this trip had proved to me. No matter how I had felt over the last years of my mother's life, the move to the farm and after her passing, finding myself so alone, I had been loved. My grandparents adored me.

I picked up my phone and pressed speed dial. It rang and then he answered.

"Talia. How are you two doing over there?"

"Dad, I'm fine, Greer is as you might imagine and I want to come home."

"You'll be home Friday. That's still the plan?"

"Yes. These people are deranged."

"I wouldn't go that far. Let's say eccentric."

"Everything makes sense now."

My father laughed. "You had to experience them for yourself. I would never have been able to convince you."

"I'm Greer's relative. They won't say my name. They won't say we're sisters."

"At least you're related. I'm not sure they ever acknowledged my participation in the creation of Greer. They did like the money I gave them very much."

"I'm sorry if this is too personal but I'm trying to put all the pieces together. Were you just an easy touch or did Victoria love you?"

"Victoria still loves me, and every now and again, she does something that reminds me why I love her. It's not the same kind of love I had for your mother but it is love," my father said. "It's not a good idea to put complicated feelings under a microscope."

There was a tap at my door. "Tal. It's me."

"Come on in."

Greer opened the door. "May I stay with you tonight?"

"On this lumpy bed? Sure. Come talk to Dad." I held out the phone to her.

Getting into bed beside me, Greer took the phone. "Dad. I shouldn't have come. They're mad."

"Not clinically," I said loud enough for him to hear.

"Yes, clinically!" Greer insisted. "Am I going to grow up to be them?"

"No!" I gave her a poke with my elbow.

"Sitting at the dinner table with drool dripping from the corner of my mouth, some rotund nurse wiping my lips with a spare diaper as I blather on about the grand old days when I used to ride to hounds."

"You've never done that," I reminded her. "But you have a very vivid imagination. Now I know where Victoria gets it from."

The sooner we got back to the farm, the better all around.

***

The following morning, we ate alone in the day room. Fifi, of course, was sound asleep. We had heard scampering and giggling down the hall late the night before. Neither of us wanted to know the details.

Greer headed out to track down Lord Rowe and I took a walk through the gardens. The newest one was Edwardian and designed by Gertrude Jekyll. I knew this because a groundskeeper was tending one of the beds and told me all about it as a point of pride. Jekyll was an unknown to me but to the gardening world, she was a big deal. Of course, this was an area they could not possibly use in the movie. Too modern by about five hundred years.

I was told that this house had been a favorite hangout for the artistic crowd in the late eighteen hundreds. One weekend, they got together to paint a mural on a wall in a third floor hallway. History, that, he said.

Any prominent family would have seen its share of other luminaries of the time.

This was a lull period for Rowe House, with the Lord and Lady aging, there was no one to throw the kind of parties once so common here. Everyone in Little Swerden was looking forward to the movie being made of Rosamund's adventures. It would be a boost for local businesses and the movie would put Little Swerden back on the map.

He was so enthusiastic about the prospects that I could only nod in agreement. All those things were true. A movie shot here would be good for the town and the publicity would bring tourists to the house.

It would hurt Greer to think of strangers tramping through her home —it would bother me to have tours going through the farm, thoughtless, careless people leaving soda cans on antique tables— but right now this wasn't her home. It was a place where she stayed for a few years. It belonged to some people she thought she knew, and maybe one day it would be hers. Then she would have control over its destiny, be its caretaker like her ancestors had been.

The groundskeeper showed me the herd of rare black fallow deer, and conveyed the importance of the estate to the various kings of England who had hunted here. Of course, there was no hunting on the estate these days.

It was a wondrous park, with gardens, fields and woodlands. Imagining that time no longer existed was easy. There were no signs of the modern world, no power-lines, no other houses for as far as the eye could see and beyond that.

But that was true for Bittersweet Farm, too. When I looked eastward in the morning, the sun was rising over the hills, the mist hanging over the pastures, and nothing else could be seen except our property. We were very fortunate that our great-grandfather had bought the farm when land had not been at a premium. Time and the winds of fortune had been kind to us. Rowe House had existed for eight or nine times longer and one had to expect there would be moments when it could have fallen out of the family's hands.

It hadn't, though, and in Lord Rowe's way, he was hanging onto it. I hoped Greer had a plan to save it that didn't involve movies, weddings and jousting tournaments but offered adequate income.

I sat on a mossy stone bench and texted Lockie. He was probably on a horse since he started early in the morning before it became uncomfortably hot to work.

The weather had been decent so far, and I hoped it held for the Miry Brook show. I had been checking the long-range forecasts since the beginning of the month. As always, it could be wet, it could be dry, cool, or hot. The night before, maybe, we would know if we had to pack rain gear.

Any extremes in weather would mean attendance would be lower, and we needed a crowd. Greer and Ellen Berlin, of the hunt club, had prepared for many horses, riders, and spectators. There were food venders, craft displays, and historians scheduled to be on the grounds. If we were all standing in the rain, it would be disappointing.

I felt the damp penetrating my jacket, so left the bench and walked toward the house. This would have been a very lonely place for one little girl to grow up. I supposed Victoria had found it to be that way, especially when her parents had spent so much time on the Continent. She had lived here with a nanny, Greer had revealed some years back and I was surprised I remembered that now.

The upper class raised children differently. Even though my father had traveled a good deal, there was no doubt that he wanted both of us with him at the farm. He could have easily sent us away to school and then to summer camps. Instead, we lived with him and went to day school in Newbury, then finally homeschooled, by our own choice, so we didn't need to leave the farm at all.

I could picture a six-year old Greer being sent away to boarding school. What had her grandparents said to her? "It's a family tradition. Tough it out, we all did." She would have raised her chin in defiance and made the best of a bad situation.

There were footsteps and I turned to see Greer jogging to catch up with me. "Walter told me you were out here. I can get a flight back this afternoon. That means we leave now."

"Are you done here?

"Yes. The movie is publicity for the house. They're going to turn it into a B&B."

"Greer."

"A hotel. My home."

We walked on together.

"Not my home, but the family seat."

"I understand."

"People will be having sex in my bed."

"I so know where Victoria gets these weird ideas from."

"My bed is a virgin!" Greer protested.

I started to laugh.

"See how I can do that to you?" She bumped against me.

"Let's leave. I've seen the place. It's beautiful. Next time they'll have a tee shirt printed 'London. Rome. New York. Little Swerden.'"

"Selling in the gift shop."

"Of course. With DVDs of Rosamund's movie."

"I'm starting to hate that woman," Greer said.

We entered the house. The movie people were gathered with the Rowes, and Fifi had managed to put herself together.

"Where have you been?" Lady Rowe asked. "We wanted to share with you our big announcement."

Another big announcement? The stable was going to be turned into a day spa?

Niall made a sweeping gesture with his arm. May I present to you Titania Dudley who will be playing Rosamund Hasart and...Fifi will be playing the king's concubine, Rosamund's arch rival," he said proudly.

The dark-haired and porcelain-skinned Titania did a proper little curtsy, while Fifi was beaming and batting her eyelashes at every male in the room.

"What does she know about acting?" Greer asked sensibly.

"I attended The London School for the Performing Arts," Fifi replied.

"Did you graduate," I asked.

"No, but I stayed almost an entire year."

I nodded at Greer and she nodded back.

"It really is time for us to go."

A tall and handsome young man stepped further into the room with a glass in his hand. "You can't go, Greer. We have so much catching up to do."

Greer froze.

10

HE APPROACHED US, leaned over, and kissed her cheek.

"You're looking well," he said.

"Talia, this is Tarrant Heath. Tarrant, this is my sister, Talia. It was a surprise to see you again, but we're on our way to the airport."

He reached out and shook my hand. "It's so nice to meet you. Greer did say something about family in America."

"Yes, that's where we are," I replied.

I knew who he was, of course, having seen his photo taking a victory lap any number of times in *The Equestrian Gazetteer*. He was one of Britain's up-and-coming show jumper riders and spent much of his time on the European circuit.

"And that's where I'll be," Tarrant said.

Greer began walking toward the exit and stopped. "In what way, that's where you'll be?"

"I'm the new trainer for Mark Kobayashi. We met in Aachen a few months ago. He was parting ways with—"

"Tyler Ott," I supplied.

"Yes. I thought it would be fun and your mother had told me you lived in that part of the States so that was a bonus. We always had such good times together. Remember..."

"No, I don't." Greer cut him off. "Sorry to run, but we do have a plane to catch."

I nodded at Tarrant and hurried after Greer.

"So—" I started.

"He was another one of my mistakes, wasn't he?" Greer opened her bedroom door and began throwing things into her suitcase.

"When?" I asked, trying to remember her last trip to England.

"When I was stupid, right?"

"He's very handsome," I said.

I could understand how anyone would be attracted to him and, for the thirty seconds I had known him, Tarrant seemed nice.

"Go pack!"

Obviously, he was of that same aristocratic class as Greer, and possessed the smooth social graces she had learned, but mostly did not use.

I went into the Sword Bedroom and began gathering my things together. Three minutes later, Greer burst in and began throwing things into my bag.

"I'm trying to be neat!"

"I'm trying to get us out of this freaking mausoleum."

"You love it! This is the house you flew three thousand miles to protect."

"Another one of my mistakes!" She glanced around the room. "Do you have everything?"

Searching around in confusion, I didn't see anything, but felt there was something else. "I don't know."

"You'll replace it!" She grabbed the bag and rushed out the door.

We hurried down the long staircase and found the group still together, chummily drinking and noshing.

"Bye," Greer said and headed for the door.

"Thank you for the very nice stay," I said to Lady Rowe. "I'll tell Victoria—"

"Talia! If you're not in the car in ten seconds, I'm leaving without you!" Greer shouted.

I shrugged. "Something."

"I'll see you in the States," Tarrant called to me as I raced away.

***

Halfway across the Atlantic, we were served a meal. It was better than what we had had since leaving home but that wasn't saying much. If we had called ahead, Jules would have made us something wonderful to celebrate our return, but Greer wanted us to say nothing. Whatever Jules was preparing for dinner would be good so I didn't think we were risking much there. If our early arrival was supposed to be a surprise, it would be. Maybe Greer wanted to see how much we were missed. After the distinctly cool greeting she had gotten from her grandparents, I'm sure a fuss would be a treat. Having been gone for only two days, it couldn't be very much of a fuss, but I was ready to be home and close to Lockie again.

Greer poked at her food, then put the napkin over it.

"He lives nearby."

"Tarrant?"

"Yes. The Heaths aren't as old a family as we are. Rather upstarts one might say."

"When did they join the exclusive club?"

"Elizabeth the First gave them the house."

"Fifteen hundreds. Hardly any time at all," I teased.

"It's bigger than ours. They've always lacked a little decorum but they have money and no strangers traipsing through the place."

"You've known him for years?"

"I knew of him," Greer replied. "He's very conspicuous. Then my grandmother started arranging parties where we would be near each other. Every year for every visit he'd be around. He was fun to be with. He had a barn full of nice horses. We rode together."

"It must have been good to get away from your grandparents for a while."

"My mother was always in London or Paris. I had to..."

"I understand. I was stuck alone, too."

"I was young. I was stupid. I thought I loved him. I thought he loved me." Greer paused. "I thought the same about each of them."

"You don't need to explain. It's okay."

"Maybe we were fond of each other a little bit." Greer looked out the window at the sky. "In a naïve way."

The minutes ticked past. "I get it now."

"I thought you might."

"Go slow. Cam will understand."

"Will he? He has quite a reputation."

"Lockie has a history, too." I opened a bag of winegums I had bought at the airport and offered Greer a candy. "Rowe House has a history. Every generation has left its mark somehow and changed it. It's matured and grown over the years. Today, it's beautiful. Everyone is partially the product of their experiences. The events we suffer

135

through act like a polishing cloth or a chisel. It's your choice of which one, but it's one or the other."

"Do you always find the good in everyone?"

"Be serious. No. I'm not that smart. Has Cam ever done anything to hurt you?"

Greer looked at me.

"Except for that horrible time he tried to comfort you in Florida."

Greer was silent.

"He's a guy. He was doing the best he could. He offered you what he had, not realizing—"

"—how wrong I'd take it."

"You had your own reputation."

"No one's ever propositioned you."

"Not that I remember," I replied.

"There's something about me..." Greer started.

"No. There's nothing about you. Never was and there isn't now. You just didn't understand you were offering these boys or men something rare and spectacular and they were too jejune to comprehend it. Cam's not like that. He knows. Give him a chance. Give yourself a chance."

"You'll always be there to pick up the pieces," Greer said without looking at me.

"Yes, I will."

***

They were just sitting down to dinner when we arrived.

Jules rushed forward to throw her arms around us as though we had been gone for months.

"What are you doing here?" She stepped back.

"It was time to come home," I said.

Jules kissed both of us. "Sit. Have you eaten? Are you hungry? Was the food terrific there?"

I sat next to Lockie and Greer sat in her place next to Cam. "If you like dates stuffed with cheese and eggs."

"Who would do that?" my father asked.

"It seems a little creative," Cap admitted. "You don't often find fruit served with whole eggs. Cheese, yes."

"They've gone medieval." Greer unfolded her napkin and put it in her lap. "It's to get into the spirit of the movie, and, by the way, Jules, your sister is playing the king's concubine."

Lockie turned to me.

"True."

"Titania Dudley is playing my ancestor, Rosamund," Greer added. "Typecasting all around."

"So shooting is going ahead," Cam said.

"Yes. It's good publicity for the motel," Greer replied.

"Excuse me," my father said. "What motel?"

"Rowe House. They're turning the place into a motel, with a neon sign out front and stained carpets."

"Greer's exaggerating. Lord and Lady Rowe will be accepting guests," I explained. "There will be jousting in the Great Hall before afternoon tea and after dinner. Guests will please keep their hands and feet on the spectator side of the ropes lest the horses trample upon them. Thank you for your cooperation."

Lockie laughed.

I speared a tomato with my fork and ate it.

***

We watched the sky darken from our terrace.

"Is there more to the story than Greer told us at dinner?"

"Lockie, Tarrant Heath was there. He's from the neighborhood and I think her grandmother invited him to cause trouble."

"Why would you think that?"

"He has nothing to do with the movie and..."

"They had a fling?"

I thought about how to explain it and gave up. "Yes. She was upset to see him. He was nice enough. Handsome."

"More so than me?"

I laughed. "Maybe."

"Silly."

"Is he good?"

"On a horse, yes. Elsewhere...I don't know. I think people have one approach to life. They do everything in the same way because it's who they are, it's the only thing they know."

"So someone who is rough and impatient on a horse..."

"That's how they are."

"Now I'll be looking at everyone and wondering."

"Don't waste your time, but it is everything you need to know about it."

I laughed. "I should take your word?"

Lockie stood and didn't reply.

Getting to my feet, I went to him. "What's going on?"

"When I went to Florida, I was fine with that. You were gone two days and I wasn't so fine with that."

"I missed you, too." I kissed his cheek. "The mosquitoes are coming out. It's Thursday. Isn't *Some Like It Cold* on?"

"The show that drags us from one ice cream shop to the next?"

"That one."

"No. Why can't we watch something interesting? A documentary on a historic event."

"Like what?"

"The invention of submarines," Lockie said.

"Okay. Fine. We'll watch that."

"That was just something—"

"—you pulled out of thin air."

"Yes. As an example."

We started walking to the backdoor.

"Tarrant Heath is coming to be the trainer for Mark Kobayashi," I said.

"Tyler Ott's leaving Far Reach?"

"Apparently."

"Unexpected," Lockie replied. "They'll probably get someone to take the equitation riders because he doesn't know anything about it. It's completely American."

I knew the young European riders didn't pursue position so relentlessly. In one way, they were better off for it, but there were benefits to being able to maintain proper form over fences. If Greer and I had spent less time posing and paid more attention to our skills, Lockie would not have had some much work to do with us. It had been an arduous year, but, looking back, I enjoyed it. "Do you know Tarrant?"

"I met him somewhere. When I was in Ireland, we brought the horses to England. I think that's when it was. It wasn't after I started working with Gesine."

One hundred percent of his focus was on dressage while in Germany. I thought the excitement of show jumping was fun, not quite a replacement for cross-country although close enough to satisfy that need, but Lockie was intellectually challenged by the discipline of dressage. I had never asked but if he could only do one, that would be his choice.

"Are you tired?" Lockie asked as we went upstairs.

"My internal clock unwound two days ago."

"Try to get back to a normal schedule. It helps."

"I might read for a while."

"If you're going to read, then I can watch—"

"What?"

He paused.

"Lockie?"

"Not cage fighting, although it could be considered militaristic. There's one of those documentary drama shows starting called *Kingdom*. It's about King Richard II and his brother, somebody or other."

"Prince John." I sat on the chair to remove my shoes.

"That's right. I must have been on a horse the day they talked about that in school."

I nodded. "We'll watch it together."

That was the point of this. Being together.

11

"YOU DIDN'T SAY how my Zuckerlumpens did for you."
I was standing in the tack room looking at the schedule Cap
made for us every day.

Lockie hoisted his dressage saddle off the rack because he
was going to be schooling Tsai. For him, even with a horse
in training to be a show jumper, dressage meant the real
thing, not just some flat work with a jumping saddle.

"They're very sweet and you've done so much good for
them. Starting with Robert Easton was no help, and they
had to relearn most of what he taught them. Poppy's fine."
Lockie paused. "I think Gincy would be happier with
dressage."

I turned to him. "I know she's a bit timid in comparison with Poppy, but I thought we were building her confidence."

"No, Tal, this is not about you. You are building her confidence. Right now, she doesn't want to do what Poppy does."

"Poppy will climb up on any horse and take any fence you tell her to get over."

"She's terrific. Gincy is more of an introvert. She enjoys the precision, the discipline of dressage. Talk to her. Ask. Maybe I'm wrong."

"Did she say she didn't want to ride at Miry Brook?"

I could imagine Gincy being unwilling to confide in me, fearing I'd be disappointed with her.

"No, I think she's looking forward to that."

"As something fun but not the goal."

Lockie nodded. "I was thinking that you could have them ride in with Buck for his dressage lessons."

I thought about it for a moment.

"I'm not taking your students away from you," Lockie added.

"You ride my horse. I'm not that territorial," I replied. "If you think they'll benefit from a change of instructors, then it's worth a try. They enjoyed the sessions with you on the cross-country course. Or at least Poppy did."

"We can try today. Buck is going to a one-day tomorrow."

"I didn't know that."

He went onto the aisle. "It's close and more for practice."

"Then Buck's going next weekend to Miry Brook." I followed him to Tsai's stall.

"Too much?" Lockie smiled.

"Maybe. What's the rationale?"

"He enjoys it and he has a lot of catching up to do. Courtesy of Peter Bouley, Buck has become a nice source of income for us. Amanda thinks he's able to concentrate better when he doesn't have so much excess energy." Lockie leaned over and kissed me. "Boys aren't girls."

"That's a hard point to argue," I replied.

"You can come with us and be his coach, too."

"I won't lie and say I would love to but. One show a month is sufficient for me and we'll have two this month. The but is Kate Cooper is coming by with her actor friend and his daughter, so I need to stay here."

Lockie led Tsai onto the aisle and we attached the cross ties. "You got out of it this time!"

"And you can't go anywhere on Sunday," I said. "We're having a birthday party for Dad."

"Was I supposed to get him something?"

"No, Greer had Day paint a watercolor of the farm from all of us. It's lovely. She's so talented. I hope the painting she donated to Miry Brook brings in a good deal of money at the auction."

"I'm sure it will with Greer publicizing the event everywhere."

I helped him tack the gelding. "When are you going to show this horse?"

"There's a show at Lake Champlain next month. I was thinking about that since Cam is going. It makes it fun for us."

"Yes, you can share a room."

Lockie didn't reply.

"You do share a room when you're on the road, right?"

"Oh yes, Talia. We certainly do."

"Lockie."

"What?" he asked innocently.

"Nothing. That's fine. I'm sure you want your privacy. I'm sure you don't want to know who was in what bed for us on this trip, either. Tarrant Heath. So much catching up to do, and like that. Girls just want to have fun." Even the Sisters Grimm. I turned to walk away. "Have a good ride."

"Silly," Lockie called.

"Yes?"

"You can't seriously doubt me."

I shrugged. "Boys will be boys. Or, maybe more precisely, men will be boys."

"That's so unfair!"

"I know."

"It's so true, though," he said, unclipping Tsai and starting to walk him outside. "As long as you know that

145

about us, I'm sure you'll accommodate our minor and major indiscretions. What can you expect from guys?"

He caught up, encircled me with his arm, and a second later, I was pressed against him.

"Is that what I should expect?" I asked.

"Yes."

"I like it."

***

Lockie let Gincy ride Beau, Poppy was on Fudge, Freddi was on Keynote and Buck was on Wingspread. We all met at the outdoor arena where Lockie had a stake, a rope, and a rake.

"Would anyone like to guess what these tools are for?"

The riders shook their heads.

Lockie drove the stake into the ground and tied the rope on it. "This rope is ten meters long." He walked out as far as the rope would allow, then dropped the rake head into the footing. "I'm going to describe a twenty meter circle because..."

"A twenty meter circle is the standard for dressage," Freddi answered.

"Correct." Lockie walked around dragging the rake which made a distinct path and he stopped where he began. "If you can't make an accurate twenty meter circle, you can't progress with dressage. This is a building block. You start by trotting the circle. Did I say pear-shaped? No. Round circle. You add difficulty as your training progresses. Is there ever a time when you graduate from doing the circle?"

Gincy raised her hand tentatively.

"Gincy," Lockie called on her.

"No," she replied. "I watched grand prix dressage on the computer, and a twenty meter circle was part of the test."

"Thank you, Gincy. That's correct and that's what we're going to work on today. You'll trot this circle, following the path so you know what round feels like, and you will bend your horse to the inside. Can anyone tell me how you bend the horse to the inside?"

Buck raised his hand. "Inside rein. Inside leg at the girth."

"And?"

"Outside rein steady, outside leg behind the girth," Freddi added.

"And you do not..." Lockie said.

"Lean?" Poppy asked.

"That's right. You transfer some of your weight to the inside hip but your upper body doesn't twist or lean to the inside."

Lockie removed the stake from the center of the circle and took everything with him to the brush jump. "Buck, you first."

Of course, Wingspread had a substantial amount of dressage training as Lockie's event horse, so as long as Buck could follow instructions, they would have an easy time of it.

Cap and I watched Buck trot the circle to the left and then to the right.

"The kid is learning how to ride," she said to me.

It was true. Buck was no longer the buckaroo he had been when he arrived. He was sitting taller in the saddle, his legs reaching down around Wing's sides and he didn't need to be reminded what the exercise was supposed to be.

I wondered if this was what Lockie looked like when he was fifteen. I wondered if seeing Buck ride his horse, made Lockie feel that something important had been stolen from him. He always said no and maybe I should take him at his word. Maybe I felt if I had been in the same position, I wouldn't be able to accept the situation with as much grace as Lockie did.

Looking into the field, I saw Butch standing in the shade with the ponies. Perhaps I should give myself more credit since I accepted Butch's retirement without much of a mourning period. Of course, we had been good friends and we were still good friends, but we had both moved on. He really liked Foxy Loxy now.

Gincy went next after Buck, and rather than being tentative, she knew exactly what she had to do and did it. This was not a new exercise for her as we had worked on

148

dressage tests for months, and I was happy to see it was beginning to come together. She was in control of her body and Beau was responding to her aids.

To see that medium pony trotting the circle, on the bit and bending nicely to the inside was so cute, I wanted to hug them. Both girls deserved to be called sugar lumps.

Poppy went next on Fudge, who knew a great deal about being a hunter pony and next to nothing about anything else. Nothing more had ever been required of him than carting one little girl or another safely around a course. She had her leg on him but he wasn't bending.

We needed to work on that, but the problem during the school year was that Aly and Poppy had limited time to spend at the barn. They came as soon as school was over but then had to get home for the family. Once school was out maybe Aly could drop the girls off, and Mrs. Hamblett could pick them up later in the day. That was something we could discuss next week.

Lockie stopped her on the circle and pressed Poppy's leg against Fudge's side, then moved her hand on the inside rein. He spoke to her, then she nodded and moved off. The result was better, but it was less her than it was the pony.

"We need a pony rider strong enough to push Fudge in the right direction," Cap commented.

"Do you know one?"

"No, but there must be someone in the state," she replied, and turned. "I have to get back to Spare. Is there anything you want me to do?"

"Not at all," I said.

After watching for a few more minutes, I left to find Greer for our afternoon ride.

***

Lockie and Cam were working with the younger horses when we went up to the house before our hack.

Jules was making bread for dinner, and looked up as we entered. "There's a change of plans this weekend."

"I don't like the sound of that," I replied.

"Try to see the logic in it before you throw a temper tantrum."

"Oh, it's something to do with my mother," Greer said as she picked Joly up for a snuggle.

"Victoria is having a Father's Day party for fathers on Sunday and she's invited us."

"We're having Dad's birthday party on Sunday," I reminded her.

Jules lightly formed the dough into the shape called a *fougasse.* "We can have it on Saturday. I talked it over with your grandparents and they will be here anyway so it's not an issue for them."

"Who are fathers?" Greer asked.

"Peter Bouley, Fitch Cooper, the actor friend of Kate's. Those are the ones I know." Jules placed a tea towel used for bread and never washed, over the dough and put it aside to rise.

"I really wanted to be with my family," Greer said.

"We'll be together tomorrow night, I promise I will make it the celebration you wished for."

"Why do we give in to Victoria?" I asked. "She wants to give a party, what's that to us?"

"It's her way to demonstrate she cares about all of us. She was married to your father."

"They were divorced. That means the end." Greer put Joly down, and opened the kitchen door to take him for a walk.

"As long as you're alive, they will be connected through you," Jules pointed out.

Greer closed the door with enough force to be considered commentary.

"It was terrible at Rowe House East," I said. "I know Greer wasn't supposed to be disappointed, but she was. And Fifi."

"Biologically, you don't get to choose your family but emotionally you do," Jules replied, as she began working on the deboning the chicken.

"Why can't we unchoose Victoria?"

"Your father doesn't want to." Jules put the bones to the side to save for stock.

I thought for a moment. "There's no chance they could get back together, is there?"

"I doubt that very much," Jules replied. "They're friends. They share a daughter."

"She's pushy."

"That's where Greer gets it from."

"No, she's motivated. That comes from the Swope side." Jules smiled. "Okay."

I heard hooves on the terrace and looked out the window. Parti was looking back at me.

"What the heck is that horse doing up here? Where's Greer?" I wrenched open the refrigerator door and grabbed a couple carrots.

"We didn't have anything like this at home," Jules said. "Only people came calling."

I opened the door slowly so as not to frighten him. It would be so easy to slip on the terrace, and be injured.

He stuck his nose inside as soon as there was enough room.

"Back up."

He smelled the carrots on me, so I broke a piece off then gave it to him as I put my hand on his chest and lightly pushed. Parti took a few steps back and somehow managed to avoid bumping into the table and chairs.

I took hold of his halter and steered him away from the house. "You don't belong up here. Let me make that clear. You have your place, we have our place."

Lockie came up the path. "What are you doing with the colt?"

"It wasn't my idea. He came up for a visit," I replied.

"How did he get out?"

"I was inside. I don't know how it happened. Where's Greer?"

"At the barn talking to Cam. That's what you want, isn't it?"

"As long as they're not shouting at each other."

"They're not shouting."

"Are they..."

"No, they're talking about this weekend's show," Lockie said as we walked the colt back to the barn. "Don't be so disappointed."

"I'm not. These things take time."

"Put the colt away then we'll walk the fence-line and you can tell me all about what takes time."

Greer rushed out of the barn. "Did you see the post that lunatic wrote?"

"What post? What lunatic?" I stopped Parti, which gave him another opportunity to see if I had anything edible on me.

"She's spewing vile comments about how oppressed we are here."

"If she had only seen our oppressors," I replied, looking from Lockie to Cam.

Greer shook her head. "I don't think she'd care."

"I care. Greer, you know the internet is a full of drunk trolls—"

"What?" Lockie asked.

"And Supernova is one of them."

"What's a drunk troll?" Cam was confused. "Is that a movie? Do they lurch around bumping into trees? If so, I need to get out more."

I shook my head. "A few months ago, I did a paper for Amanda based on scientific research that said when some people are behaving badly on the Internet, their brains exhibit the same characteristics as if they were pickled in alcohol. Drunk. Troll. Drunk troll. It's a real syndrome."

"And it's a real Tweet being retweeted."

"Ignore her." I started walking the colt to the lower barn. "In twenty-four hours, it'll be old news."

"What are you doing with my horse?" Greer called.

"He came up to the house looking for you."

∾ 12 ∾

THE DAY STARTED EARLY and the mist was still hanging over the fields as I watched Lockie drive out with Wingspread in the van and Buck in the cab with him. Pete Bouley had been unavoidably detained in Tokyo but he had assured Buck he would make it to the event grounds. I hoped so for Buck's sake but I knew he was just as happy staying overnight with the Coopers. Fitch was home for the fake holiday, and Kerwin would be able to attend Victoria's gathering.

Cap passed me as she led two horses out to the field. "If you could spot me on Spare later this morning that would be good."

"You're still going to Miry Brook?" I called after her.

"Of course. And Mackay will be there."

I followed her. "Are you—"

"No. I'm nowhere near over Mill, but that doesn't mean I don't like company. Mackay will probably be in London by September. There may be a job opening there that suits his talents better than anything here. I don't know what it is. Financial something. He can do math like you wouldn't believe."

Opening the gate, I waited for her to go through with the horses then carefully unclip the lead ropes. They walked a few steps away then trotted up the rise.

"Have you heard from Mill? Heard anything about him?"

"That wouldn't be a good idea. One thing I learned from my mother is to accept it's over when it's over. She gave my father enough leeway he was able to have another family. When he began spending so much time away from us, she should have made it clear he should act like a husband and father or it was over."

"Isn't something like that hard to call?"

"No. That's why they have private detectives."

I laughed. "You think your mother should have hired someone to follow him?"

"Yes."

"She didn't suspect him," I replied.

"Why not? He was hardly ever home. That should have been a red flag."

"I'm not saying this to hurt your feelings but you were completely blindsided by Mill breaking up with you, isn't that true?"

"What an idiot."

"No, you're not."

"Not me, him!"

"I agree. Come up to the house for breakfast. Jules was making blueberry muffins when I was there."

***

Around 9:30, I got a call from Lockie saying Buck had nailed the dressage test and they were about to walk the cross-country course. He met someone he knew from before who wanted a coach in preparation for a trial in July and Lockie agreed to do that.

I clicked off, then Greer and I went to the outside course to pop over the fences then take a walk in the woods before the flies became a torment. We made plans to get finished with all our work early in order to be able to help Jules with our own party.

"Maybe we should have made reservations," she said, as we walked along the trail.

"Don't you think it's difficult for a restaurant to accommodate a dozen people at one table?"

"That's why we aren't going out, because they can't do their job?"

"That's partially the reason. Your group takes up so much space, you can't talk to whoever is at the other end of the table, your chairs are bumping into someone behind you. I don't enjoy it. Too many people."

"Isn't it about what Dad wants?"

"Why would he want to go out? Why are you so cranky?"

"I don't like Supernova and I read in *The Gazetteer* that Tarrant will be at Far Reach by mid-July."

"What's that to us?" I asked.

"Anytime you think that something isn't going to impact your life, then it does. I didn't think Supernova would be a problem when I agreed to do a simple little interview with her, did I?"

"No, but I don't see how a couple stupid Tweets impacts us. Those things go by so fast."

"It's like she's obsessed with me."

"To know you is to be obsessed with you," I replied.

"Tal, this is serious!"

"I think she is obsessed with the activism meme and the side-saddle competition fits nicely. That's all it is. She'll rant and rave."

"Everything on the Internet is forever."

"To be replaced with other stupid ideas. Within a year there have been a billion tweets burying you."

"Have you ever heard of Google? Type my name in and I'll be called a corset-wearing repressed Edwardian."

"Don't talk like that around Cam," I suggested.

"Why not?"

"Corset. That's an image he won't be able to get out of his mind. Everything you've said that Supernova considers a downside, Cam and Lockie would consider it the reverse. Trust me on this."

"No."

"When Cam saw you in the riding habit, fabric falling gracefully to the ground, nipped in the waist, the white frilly stock-tie at the neck, it made a big impression on him. Huge."

"Is this true?"

"Yes, Greer," I said honestly.

"Why?"

"Are you serious?"

"Of course."

"He thinks you're beautiful."

"Well, of course. They all did."

"Don't dismiss his feelings like that. It's real for him. You're not looking at Cam when he's looking at you. You keep your eyes down so you miss his expression."

Greer didn't say anything.

"If you want to ignore him, that's your choice but I think you run a risk."

"Which is?"

"He may give up. You should have heard Cap go on about knowing when to cut your losses. It was scary how practical she can be."

"She just got dumped."

We reached the stream and the horses lowered their heads to drink.

"I wouldn't quite put it that way."

"Broke up with no rejoining in sight," Greer revised.

"People do move on. They get tired of being rebuffed."

"I don't know if I'm ready."

"Then tell him so he can get on with his life."

CB pawed the stream, splashing hard enough that I felt the water on my face. Picking up the reins so he didn't feel free to roll, I urged him forward.

"That would be a personal conversation," Greer said, following me toward the barn.

"You can do it."

I couldn't get over the sense that Cam would be so good for her, but I didn't want him holding onto false hope. If Greer genuinely couldn't take the next step, she needed to be sensitive to Cam's feelings.

Maybe he would just find a length-of-the-show-season girlfriend, or rekindle the relationship with the rider whose name I could never remember. Maybe Cam was fine with no one special in his life. He was busy between Bittersweet and Acadiana, showing nearly every weekend. Having a relationship could be a complication he didn't need now, either.

Friends and nothing more might be just the right arrangement for Greer and Cam now. It would be better for everyone if they worked it out soon. Being tentative was never good because no one could steer a parked car.

***

Shortly after lunch, Kate found us in the barn, trimming manes.

"Hi, Talia. This is Ami Gish."

She was a slight, pretty girl with short brown hair, big brown eyes and lightly tanned skin. If she rode with us all summer, that would change.

I stepped off the bucket. "Hi, Kate. Hi, Ami. How are you?"

"I'm fine. It's nice to meet you. This is a beautiful farm."

"Thank you. We like it. Did you bring your riding clothes?"

"Yes..."

"Why don't we get you on our pony, Oh Fudge, and I can get an idea of where you are. We have two pony riders. They would love to have someone join them. They are a little younger than you are, I suspect. Are you thirteen?"

"I was fourteen in April."

161

"Fudge will take good care of you today, and then maybe you can switch to Keynote."

While Ami rushed off to change, Cap and I brought Fudge out of his stall. I helped tack him and chatted with Kate. She told me they were looking forward to Victoria's party, the last one had been so invigorating. Cam wouldn't make it back from Ohio in time, but the rest of the Cooper clan would be there.

I asked about Pete Bouley.

Kate shrugged. "He doesn't understand that when you make a promise to your family, you need to keep it."

"Most people don't understand that. I hope Buck isn't hurt."

"I suspect he knows what his parents are like by now. We enjoy him. Buck can stay with us for as long as he needs a place but shuttling between the two homes isn't a stabilizing situation."

"There's always the emancipated minor route if things get bad enough," I replied.

"Then he can stay with us. I wouldn't like to see him on his own."

"He's been on his own already," I said in agreement.

"My kids were never on their own. I think that's why Cam kept going off with that pony—to get away from me."

I was going to refute that but decided to be honest. "Probably. That's Cam."

"And how is Greer?"

"Busy."

Ami returned wearing jodphurs and boots and carrying her helmet. As we went to the ring, I asked about her experience, what she had been doing in the riding program in school, and what she would like to accomplish this summer.

She didn't have the kind of experience I hoped for, telling me that there were so many girls and not enough horses to ride every day. If a rider had one hour on a horse three times a week, not much progress will be made. Hours in the saddle is what makes a difference, in addition to challenges beyond going around and around in a ring.

"Fudge will take good care of you." I gave her a leg up.

The overall picture was acceptable, but Ami wasn't tight in the saddle. There was room under her knee and the position of her foot in the stirrup wasn't giving her a proper base of support. Call would be too advanced for her as he needed a rider who had a strong will. Fudge was accustomed to riders like Ami, a little delicate, a bit tentative, and somewhat unsure about herself.

I had her walk, trot and canter both directions, then trot over a few low fences.

"I don't know that much about riding, although Cam has tried to get me on a horse and I gave in a few times. I have watched him, though," Kate said. "Ami has a lot of work ahead of her."

"Not everyone who rides wants to become as accomplished as Cam."

"You think he's good?"

"Cam is a wonderful rider, and I don't say that lightly. Given how the emphasis is on winning at any cost for many of the top tier riders, it's not easy to fit into the philosophy of Bittersweet Farm where the horse comes first, and he does."

Kate smiled proudly. "I love that kid."

"You did a good job with him."

"Thank you, but it was him."

It made me want Cam in the family even more.

"So, Ami. Would you like to ride here this summer?" I asked.

"Yes, I would."

∾ 13 ∿

BY THE TIME GREER AND I REACHED THE
HOUSE after all our chores, Lockie called to say the cross-
country phase had gone very well and Buck would be riding
in the show jumping soon. The competition in his division
was about what he had expected. The riders were at Buck's
level but Wingspread was much more experienced than
most of the other horses.

Buck just had to stay on and steer with Wing. It was a
good introduction to combined training for him but
somewhat unrealistic. I didn't say that because it was
obvious.

That inexperienced riders with financial resources went
out and bought made horses was nothing new. It could be

argued that Nicole bought Obilot who was far more accomplished than she was in order to have predictable wins in the hunter ring. Her equitation horse was push-button and gave her a very high opinion of her abilities that were undeserved.

I hoped Nicole would find the right combination of uncomplicated horse and very patient trainer who would take her money but not take advantage of her. At least not too egregiously.

***

As I was about to get into the shower, Lockie called. Buck had placed fourth in the trial and was very pleased. Mr. Bouley hadn't shown up which was no surprise to Buck and he didn't seem unhappy about it.

They were on their way home. Lockie understood that there was a birthday party this evening and he assured me they would be home in plenty of time. I told him not to rush, that it was better to arrive late but safely.

I was pulling a dress on over my head when my grandmother knocked on my door.

"Talia. Are you decent?"

"Very," I replied, straightening the fabric.

"Isn't that pretty?" She said. "You're a lovely girl, and you should dress up more often."

I laughed.

"I had to say that, I'm your grandmother. You'd rather be wearing boots, I know."

"It's what you're accustomed to," I said. "Working all day with the horses, I can't be wearing heels and a pencil skirt."

"I'll have to talk to Andrew about this. Why he's making you do all that work is beyond me."

"He's not. It's my choice."

The door opened and Greer entered. "Do you want me to do your hair? Hi, Gram."

"Sure, that would be good."

"Victoria said you had a visit with her parents this week."

Greer reached for my comb. "Is she here?"

"She stopped by to drop off a gift for your father and has gone home now to prepare for tomorrow. That's a woman who knows how to give a party."

I heard Greer sigh.

"Tell me all about the charity work for the show next weekend," my grandmother said, making herself comfortable in the chair.

By the time Greer had braided my hair, she had finished making a full report on Miry Brook and we all went downstairs. Cap and Jules were completing all the preparations, then left us to take over while they changed.

"Where's Dad?" Greer asked.

"He and your grandfather went for a walk to talk."

"About whether or not Dad should run for office?" I asked.

"That's probably part of it. Is there anything we can do to prepare for our party?"

"That was quite a topic change," Greer commented.

"It's a father and son talk. Business, politics, you two."

My grandmother wasn't going to give anything away and while I went to the refrigerator to see what was in there that should come out, I saw the van drive to the barn.

"Greer, can you hold down the fort? Lockie just came back." I went to the door, took off my shoes, and pushed my feet into the wellies waiting there.

"We're done at the barn!" She called after me as I hurried out the door, sure my grandmother despaired of me ever becoming a proper lady.

I reached the van as they were letting the ramp down and Buck ran up to get Wing.

"Everything went well?" I asked.

"I'd say. There were three other riders a little smoother around the edges than he was today, but that's no big deal."

"We'll get some sand paper," Buck said, grinning as he brought Wing to the ground. "I'll take good care of Mr. Wing and you can get to the party."

"I'll get cleaned up, check on you, then you can change and come up to the house and join us."

Buck shook his head. "I wouldn't...I'm not family. I'll be fine here."

"You'll come up to the house and celebrate with the rest of us," I said, leaving no room for uncertainty.

Lockie and I started up the drive.

"I know his father's busy but he sure isn't off to a very good start with the parenting role," I said. "He was better off with the Coopers."

"I can't disagree with you there," Lockie replied.

He went to the carriage house and I returned to help Jules with our feast.

It was such a different atmosphere than Rowe House East, although wildly eccentric Grandpa Rowe did seem to be laughing and enjoying himself quite a bit. I wasn't sure he had a reason but he was having fun.

Greer had Joly in her arms so I knew she was thinking and feeling too much. I went to her and suggested we give Joly dinner so he wouldn't be so preoccupied with our food.

"I'm glad you have something to compare this to now," she said as we fixed a bowl full of everything Joly liked. "You didn't see my grandfather's car."

"Is it a Rolls?"

"No, it's his grandfather's car. A Runciman Rajah. It's so old it's almost impossible to get parts for it. It's not even a convertible. It never had a top. It practically spits fire out the exhaust pipe when it goes down the road. Our...their other car is a Rolls. It's not so embarrassing."

I put my arm around her. "No wonder you wanted the old pickup truck."

"I love it."

That was the truck Cam found for her.

"Come on, you two. Join the family," my grandmother called to us.

***

We sat around the table, plates full of food arriving and leaving empty as we told tall tales until the mosquito candles stopped working. My father loved the painting of the farm that Day had created for him, swore he'd wear the tie with hunting horns on it, assured us that the book we had found was just the one he'd wanted for ages. The cake Jules had made was a triumph and there was nothing left but crumbs.

With another party facing us the next day, we called it a night, put the leftovers away, and cleaned up the mess.

My father and grandfather went into the den to have a brandy and cigar, not talked out yet. Or perhaps it was settled and they were just relaxing now that a decision had been made.

I thought everyone's role had shifted. Before this offer to run for office, I didn't have opinions about what my father should do with his life. Of course, I wanted him to be happy and successful but since he seemed to be, I never thought about it. Now I was thinking about his life.

Wanting the best for him, I was biased against a public life, but I kept that opinion to myself. It was just an opinion, there was no research to back it up. How would you be able to foretell the future anyway?

My father had been very understanding when I had needed to make my own choices over the past few years. While we might have discussed situations, he never told me what to do. I think he trusted me to be wise. I wanted to trust in his wisdom to do what was right for himself, the family, and the community.

Still, I was very concerned. Over the past year, we had all come together at the farm. That intimacy we shared was precious and I didn't want to lose it.

I thought I might be a little selfish but wasn't sure. If my father chose to become a public figure, I would learn to deal with it. Time apart is a reminder to value the time together. I would make those moments count, the way we had celebrated his birthday, grateful he was in our lives.

***

"Thank you for bringing me into your family, Talia," Lockie said as we entered the carriage house.

"You're welcome and I mean that you are welcome not that I had much to do with it."

"It would be a different situation if we hadn't..."

"You would still be the trainer, you would still eat all your meals at the house, you would still live on the property."

"In the hay loft with the ugliest sofa in the world."

"You think Dad built this house because of me? Think again. He built it because he knew you were here permanently." With a sigh of relief, I took off my girl shoes. "We needed extra storage space anyway."

"Let me know when you plan on bringing boxes over."

"You'll be helping to carry them." I headed up the stairs.

"I'm being serious, Silly. Thank you."

"It's kind of a crazy family so I'm not sure what you see in us."

He put his arms around me. "You should have come to the event today."

"Did you need someone to hold Wing?"

He nuzzled my neck. "You always think up the best comebacks."

∽ 14 ∾

BY ELEVEN, we were on the cross-country course having a group session in preparation for Miry Brook.

"There are no set number of strides between fences, correct?"

We all nodded.

"I can't hear your heads rattling," Lockie said.

"You can't count the strides," Cap answered for the rest of us.

"Okay. So when you're six strides away from the fence, what do you do?"

"Throwing the reins at him works for me," I replied.

"It's wonderful to believe that your horse can see the distance when you're riding an outside course but, unfortunately, that's not how it works. How many feet is six strides? In general."

"Six times twelve," Greer replied.

"How many feet do we allot in front of a jump."

"Six feet before, six feet after," Buck answered.

"Right. Eighty feet out, approximately, we need to be able to make any adjustments necessary. Those eighty feet are going to go under us very quickly. What's eighty feet look like?" Lockie stood in front of us with a hundred foot long tape measure in his hand. "Tell me how to move. Closer to the jump or farther away."

We spent the next several minutes disagreeing about where eighty feet was.

Finally, I urged CB forward to stand on the line in front of the fence. "This is six strides," I said.

"You're sure?" Lockie asked.

"At CB's hand gallop."

Poking the end of the tape measure into the ground by CB's hoof, he walked to the fence, letting the tape stream out behind him. He stopped in front of the logs. "This is six strides. Talia has a very good eye. She knows her horse." Lockie reeled the tape measure back in. "By the time you hit the point where CB is standing, you have to commit to the fence. You have to feel your speed, the length of the stride, how fast you're covering ground and make the adjustment. Don't wait until you get closer because?"

"You can throw the horse off balance," Buck replied.

"I don't want to fuss fuss fuss all the way down to the jump. I want to see the distance, make any adjustment necessary, maintain support for my horse, and take the fence."

Greer looked up. "You see it at shows all the time. Half halt, half halt three strides out."

"What happens?"

"Rail down," she replied.

"You don't want to make the horse compensate for you. Ride quietly."

"What if you have a really strong horse?" Freddi asked.

"What do you think the answer is?"

She thought for a moment. "I know what the common answer is. Stronger bit. But I'm going to say go back to basics."

"That would be my inclination. Horses rush for a reason. We don't want to create conditions where the horse becomes stressed and panicky, or overly enthusiastic. We want to ride quietly but firmly, assuring the horse that we know what we're doing."

Buck laughed. "Even if we don't."

"That's right," Lockie replied. "You're all going to take this fence. I want you to hand gallop, get to six strides out, and make any corrections you feel are required to take the jump safely and in a hunterly fashion. Miry Brook is a hunter show, not cross-country. Tal, you go first and show them how it's done."

CB was strong and enthusiastic, but that willingness made him a very easy ride. All that was required was to keep him in a frame, maintaining firm contact with the reins and light contact with the saddle. Ears pricked forward, he seemed happy with life. We took the jump, looped back and stopped in front of Lockie.

"Very nice. Who's next?"

***

I was buttoning up a crisp cotton camp shirt I had chosen to wear at the Father's Day festival at Rowe House Farm. With teal trousers, it was the kind of simple outfit I had always defaulted to. Jules and Greer would wear summer dresses fit for a garden party, but since I was not attending entirely of my own free will, there was no point in over-doing the prep work.

"Silly." Lockie left the bathroom fresh from his shower. "I would like to say something you probably don't want to hear."

"Oh, fantastic! Really put me in the party mood."

Lockie crossed to the dresser, found one of his good polo shirts, and pulled it on. "Forget it then."

"No, you started. Say it."

"When I say something I want it to be well-received. You've already decided it's something bad."

"You said I wouldn't want to hear it."

"You won't."

I pushed my feet in my good paddock boots. We were going to be on the lawn and stylish shoes with spiky heels get stuck in the turf. I just wanted to walk without extracting my shoe with each step.

"Say it!"

"You're a really good rider."

I looked at him.

He looked back inquisitively.

"What does that mean?"

"You need that translated?"

"Good in comparison to the girls in the 4-H Club?"

He shook his head as he put his socks on.

"Do you see any trophies in the den with my name on them?"

"No."

"*Res ipsa loquitor*," I said.

Lockie slid his belt through the belt loops of his trousers. "The thing doesn't speak for itself. I'm telling you. Who are you going to believe, a judge or me?"

I couldn't think of how to answer that without digging myself deeper.

"I watch you every day on all the horses, with their different personalities, quirks and experience levels. You adapt to each without a fuss and ride with...sensitivity," he said. "Don't glare at me. This is a compliment, not a criticism."

"This was not an opinion I needed to hear."

"An opinion? From me? You don't need to hear it?"

"We're going to be late."

He caught my hand as I was going past, and didn't let go. "What would be so bad about being so good?"

"You can't understand that?"

"No."

"I'll explain it to you."

Lockie sat on the bed, not releasing his grip on my hand. "All ears."

"Because if I'm so good, I'm failing."

Lockie nodded. "I didn't think I needed this explained, but you just proved me wrong. What the heck are you talking about?"

"In the Margolin family all I heard growing up was 'Don't hide your light under a bushel. Stand tall.' In the old country, you had to be careful. Being good meant you turned yourself into a target but when my family arrived in America, that was different. There were no soldiers patrolling the streets and looking for someone who thought too well of themselves. Margolin. Yes. Achievement oriented. No lights under bushels for us."

"I'm struggling here, Tal. Help me out."

"Everyone has always told me how accomplished I am. Smart, talented, pretty even. I was given these gifts and I couldn't do the work at The Briar School. We were homeschooled and quit. I have routinely placed no better than third in any show for five years. I can't run a charity like the Swopes find so easy to do. If you tell me I'm a talented rider, there is only your bias, like that of my grandparents and mother. In the real world, I still place third."

"It didn't occur to you to tell me this?" Lockie asked.

"Why would I confess this unless under duress? I'm ashamed of my ineptitude."

Lockie paused. "I'm trying not to take this personally and you'll be glad to know I'm almost entirely succeeding. I'll just say one thing. To come in contact with you, is to have your life improved. That goes for people and horses. You can tell me I'm biased, but it's the truth." He let my hand go.

"I annoy people!"

"Yes, you do." Lockie laughed.

"What's such an improvement about that?"

"You saved Greer's life. You probably saved mine. I would have gone back to eventing."

"Even though the doctor told you not to?"

"My first doctor said to be careful. It was Dr. Jarosz, who you found for me, who explained why this would not have been a good idea. But, Tal, I had nothing after the accident. I couldn't get a job. I had no money, no horse. I had to go back to what I knew how to do. Because of you, and your family, I did. So, think about that good you've done. And, of course, you're going to win your hunter division at Miry Brook. Then you can stop complaining that you always come in third."

"It's not about ribbons."

"Did you know I didn't live with Jennifer?" Lockie stood and began walking out of the bedroom.

"No, I thought you did."

"Unh uh. You're the only person I ever wanted to live with."

He started down the stairs.

"Even though you are kind of crazy," he added.

"Lockie!"

***

Rowe House couldn't have looked more beautiful, with tended gardens, flowers bursting with color like a spilled paintbox, and broad expanses of perfectly mown lawn. Roll the Dice and Whiskey were out to pasture wearing fly sheets and face masks.

I took a quick walk through the barn and could see that Tracy and Greg were doing an excellent job. If he wanted a second chance, this was his best opportunity to begin to redeem himself. In a few years, most people would have forgiven or forgotten that problem with the commissions, and he could go back to the jumper world.

This seemed a nice enough way to live, on a lovely estate without many demands. Greg certainly didn't have to worry about paying for hay or the vet, the way he did when running his stable.

As I walked out of the barn, Greg drove into the yard on the farm tractor.

"Hi, Talia." Greg swung down to the ground. "How's that pony working out for you?"

"He's a sweetheart," I replied. "The place looks wonderful."

"Thank you. It's a good place. Tracy and I like it. It's small enough for us to handle everything. She rides, I ride, and Victoria rides Dice nearly every day."

"Really?"

"Yes. There are trails. Sometimes we all go out together and sometimes she goes out alone. I try to keep track of the time. Don't want to lose her out there!" He smiled. "She's been generous to us, and I want to return the favor."

"I'm sure you are. I'm happy for you. Where's Tracy now?"

"Up at the house with the caterer. She learned a lot from Jules, so can help out. I'm sure you'll see her. Go on up and enjoy the food. It's delicious. I snuck a taste and got my hand slapped but it was worth it."

"I'll see you later. Come up and talk to Lockie."

Greg shrugged uncertainly.

"Really. It'll be fine," I said, heading up to the house.

The party was being held on the patio, with urns spilling over with flowers, and candles and lanterns placed strategically around for light when needed later. A large table was situated to one side, covered with a colorful Provençal tablecloth, and several platters with one-bite creations that looked like miniature works of art.

"Where were you?" Greer asked coming up to me.

"The barn. I saw Greg."

"I saw Tracy in the house. She seems happy. Can we go now?"

"Have you seen your mother?"

"No."

"You will now."

Greer turned to the French doors and Victoria stepped outside, with Pete Bouley just inches away.

"Don't tell me that's her new boyfriend," Greer said.

I had that impression, too, but I wasn't going to say anything about it. "They just walked out of the house together. Let's not jump to conclusions."

"Then you don't know my mother very well."

I bumped Greer with my hip as Victoria approached.

"Thank you for coming to the Father's Day party, and thank you for bringing your father."

"Our pleasure," I said for lack of anything else to say.

"And it's nice to see you finally got back into the country, Mr. Bouley," Greer said.

"Yes, the flight I was supposed to take was cancelled and then we had a lay-over. International travel is difficult."

Greer looked at me. "We managed to get to London and back this week with no trouble."

Pete ignored the comment. "I'm sorry I missed Buck's horse show, but there will be others."

"Maybe you'll make the one this coming weekend," Victoria inserted before Greer had a chance to respond.

"One this weekend? I was supposed to go to Bangalore."

"We're all riding in the show," Victoria replied.

"You, too? Maybe Bangalore can wait. I'd like to see you all doing...whatever it is you do."

"I'm sure Buck would be happy to explain everything to you. Oh, look. The Coopers just arrived," Greer said and dragged me away.

"Poor kid," I said.

"I know what it's like and it's not going to work out."

"It's none of our business," I replied. "I feel bad about it but we've done all we can."

Greer stopped. "I don't believe you just said that."

"It's a family issue. We'll keep an eye on him this summer and come September, he might want to make other arrangements. He'll be sixteen soon."

"And?"

"He knows we're there for him. If you don't think he does, ask him. Then it won't be on your mind."

"Happy Father's Day," I said as we stepped closer to Kate and Fitch. "Where's Kerwin?"

"In the house searching for a slice of orange for his drink," Kate replied. "So. Pete's dating Victoria?"

Greer made a face at me.

"I'm asking. They seem pretty cozy."

"Kate," Fitch started.

She leaned closer to me. "We don't mind having Buck with us, but Pete came straight here from the airport. I'm not making any insinuations."

"Not much," Fitch replied. "I'm going to see what's taking the food so long to arrive."

"There are noshes over there." Kate pointed to the table.

Fitch walked away. "I want food. This is my day, I should be having beer and pizza, not a tasting a menu."

"We could go to Antonio's afterward," Greer said.

"What a good suggestion," Kate replied.

We talked for a few minutes more, then Jules, my grandparents and Dad came over. Finally, the food started to arrive and it was excellent. There was no need to go to Antonio's, and even Fitch didn't miss going for pizza.

⚮ 15 ⚮

BECAUSE SCHOOL WAS NOW OFFICIALLY OVER, Aly Beck dropped off the Zuckerlumpens in the morning. The ponies had been fed, but now the girls would assume full care of them whenever they were spending the entire day at the farm. Under Cap's watchful eye, they groomed their ponies while I had a training session on Kyff and Greer rode Bria.

"Kyff's had five months off," Lockie started. "Do you think we should take him to a show?"

"I wish..." I half-passed by him, "Poppy was tall enough to show him."

"Why?" Greer asked.

"Because she could ride him in equitation and the pressure would be less. He can pop over the fences, laze around the ring, snore as he goes in front of the judge."

"I don't know that she can handle him," Greer said. "Nicole couldn't."

I pulled Kyff up, took the phone from my pocket and clicked speed dial. "Hi, Cap. Would you send Poppy to the ring with her helmet? Thanks." I clicked off. "Maybe I'm wrong. We'll stand by the track and catch him if he hurtles past us out of control."

"Usually a judge wants to see a rider appropriately mounted. The horse and rider should fit each other. Poppy rides a pony for a reason," Lockie said.

"I'm just saying that it would be better for him. She could show him in children's hunters."

"If it wasn't even noon yet, I would explain this idea by saying you'd been in the sun too long without a hat." Greer came to a halt next to me.

I dismounted as Poppy ran into the ring.

"Hi! Are you going to let me ride one of the big horses? Which one? Kyff?" Poppy pushed the helmet onto her head.

"Yes. You're not concerned about it, are you?" I stood ready to give her a leg up.

"Gosh, no!"

Boosting her into the saddle was easier than lifting a bale of hay.

"He's tall," she said, picking up the reins while I shortened her stirrup leathers.

"You'll need to work those legs of yours or he won't realize you're there."

Poppy patted his neck. "We'll be fine. What are we going to jump?"

"You'll work him on the flat first and then we'll decide if you'll do anything else."

"Okay," Poppy and Kyff trotted off. "This is great!"

I had her trot and canter in both directions. While I was keeping an eye on her, I lowered the jumps to two feet.

"Walk and bring him to me."

"Talia. Let me keep riding him. Please!"

"Good luck with this, Dr. Frankenstein," Lockie said softly.

"You're going to pop him over the low fences. The low ones. You're clear on that?"

"Yes, Talia." Poppy was grinning.

"Do an egg roll course. Take the two jumps at the bottom of the ring, two on the side, the two at the top of the ring, then the two on the far side."

"I know."

"I'm just reminding you. If, at any time, he gets too strong or you feel uncomfortable, pull up."

"Yes, Talia."

"What are you going to do if he won't stop?"

"I'll turn him in a small circle. A horse can't run away with you if his nose is on your toe."

I patted her leg. "That's right, Good Girl. Trot. Canter a circle and start your course."

Poppy trotted happily away.

Lockie stepped closer to me. "You're going a good job with your *Zuckerwuerfel*."

"They make it easy."

Kyff went into his slow canter and took the first fence.

"I wish Nicole was here to see this," Greer commented.

Poppy started her turn.

"Inside leg," I called to her.

"He can't feel her. The flap of the saddle is too long."

"Of course he can," I replied. "Close those legs. Good. Look for your next fence."

Poppy, with her head up, and Kyff, with his head up, cantered in what seemed to be slow motion around the ring, popping over the fences that were in the way.

Course completed, Poppy dropped her reins and threw her arms around his neck. "You're such a good boy!"

"Mr. Babysitter," Lockie commented. "Lunatic in Florida, comes here and is transformed. Wait a minute, how did that happen? Oh yeah, Talia lobbied for him. One could say she changed his life."

As we all left the ring, I gave him a look and he winked back at me.

While Poppy and Cap led Kyff into the barn, Aly Beck came up to me. "I want to thank you for all you've done for Poppy. She can ride."

"That she can," Lockie agreed as he kept walking.

"She's a sweet girl and you've raised her well."

Aly smiled at me with some embarrassment. "And there I was trying to compliment you."

"Thank you. I always enjoy being with her and Gincy. They're both going to do well this weekend."

"I'm bringing the video camera so we can record it for posterity," Aly replied.

I smiled. "She'll appreciate that in the future."

I would have.

***

Lockie and I had lunch at the carriage house, sitting outside, not talking, just enjoying the summer day.

"I don't want to live with my father," Buck said coming around the side of the house. "He doesn't want to live with me. You can see how important I am to him. He couldn't even get here from Hong Kong."

"Did you have lunch?" Lockie asked.

Buck shook his head.

"Go into the house, wash up, and lunch is in the refrigerator."

Jules had made the most delicious pulled brisket sandwiches, and there was a lightly dressed tomato salad with fresh basil. We had left her, and my father, on the terrace, while Greer ate at her desk in an effort to catch up with all her work. With the show just days away, I had imagined that there was nothing left to do, but she insisted that wasn't the case. There are always last minute emergencies that need to be handled, she said.

Buck returned with a plate and a sandwich.

"What do you want to do?" I asked.

"I want to go back to the Coopers. They like me."

"I'm sure your father likes you."

"Sure?" Buck challenged.

"Not everyone is born knowing how to parent," Lockie said. "Like so many things in life, it's something you learn. Your father hasn't had much practice at it."

"And you're not a little boy," I added.

Buck took a huge bite of the sandwich. "What does that mean?"

"You're very independent," I said. "You managed to get here from Kentucky on your own. Maybe your father doesn't feel as though you need him."

"I don't."

"You're going to be here at the farm most of the time between riding and summer school until September. Can we avoid creating difficult situations and hurt feelings?

We'll discuss options, and decide what's best as we go along. Does that make sense?"

Lockie nodded at me.

"I don't want to be in that house. When he's there, he's not there. When he's not there, he has his people watching me."

"Creepy," I said.

"Way creepy."

"Stick it out," Lockie told him. "You're not a kid anymore and this is not the worst thing that will ever happen to you. We'll see if Cam can bring you to some away shows and you can help him, but you'll have to behave. No temper tantrums like this one. When Cam is showing, it's his job. He can't be trying to find your pacifier and take care of the horses, too."

Buck grinned. "I'm a little big for a baa-baa."

"Yes, you are. Make sure you act like it," Lockie replied.

"I have a lesson with the pony riders, this afternoon. If you want to ride in with them, you're more than welcome. There's a new student, too. Ami Gish. She'll need some help to get going so if you could keep an eye out for her like you do with the pony riders, that would be very good."

"Sure."

I stood up. "You boys can gossip about Sledge the Hammer..."

Lockie looked at me curiously.

"And I will go see if Greer needs any help."

"We'll be up in a while," Lockie replied.

"Okay. No figure-four leglocks while I'm gone."

"Wrestling's not on now," Buck pointed out.

"You, too?" I asked walking toward the driveway.

Greer was in her office and upset when I opened the door.

"They have a hashtag."

I sat down. "Who does?"

"The Stepford Witches."

"Nova?"

"Of course. #BanAllTheMaleThings."

"It's a little too long to remember easily. What does it mean?"

"Right now, it means ban side-saddle riding because it's a symbol of our male oppression."

"How do you ban something like that?"

"I don't know, but it's good publicity for their so-called cause."

"So what?" I asked.

"They're coming to the show."

"A couple two three of her closest friends?"

"You need a crowd to protest and get on the news."

"Wait, what?"

"Objective Miry Brook Hunt Club. They're coming in full attention-getting regalia."

"Greer, how do you know all this?"

"It's trending on Twitter." She spun the laptop around so I could see the screen.

I read a little, then quit. "They're not going to waste a perfectly good summer day on something as nonsensical as this."

"Yes, they will," Greer assured me.

***

By the time I reached the indoor, Gincy was on Beau, Poppy was on Tango, Ami was on Fudge and Buck was on Bijou. They were all trotting briskly on the track, except Ami who was barely going faster than a jog.

"Wake him up, Ami," I called. "Getting the blood moving and increasing the oxygen supplied to the muscles helps prevent injuries. It also aids in flexibility. Pick up the pace."

I watched for several strides and there was no change. "Close your legs on him."

"We're going fast enough."

Cap turned to me. "That's not a good attitude."

"Okay. It'll just take you longer to warm-up than the rest of the group but that's fine with me."

"New style," Cap said. "Bury your knuckles in the horse's neck."

Ami's over-all position was good, but the details weren't. I had the feeling I would be repeating myself all summer. Hands up. Hands up. Hands up. And I didn't want to become that kind of instructor.

If Ami didn't get her hands off Fudge's neck, she would be very limited in the use of her rein aids. If she couldn't or wouldn't get after him with her legs, Ami was no more than a mannequin.

The three other riders in the ring were well-beyond her in theory. They at least knew what they were supposed to do even if they couldn't quite put all the pieces together yet.

"How much dressage work did you do at Deacons Hall," I asked her.

"We don't do dressage," she replied, trotting slowly while Fudge swished his tail lazily back and forth.

If it was Call, he'd be laughing to himself "I've GOT her!" Two minutes later, he'd gallop her out of the arena.

I had the group reverse, trot in the opposite direction. Then they cantered. Three were at a working canter, while Fudge loped along like a little cow pony.

"Pick up his head," I said.

"How do I do that?" Ami replied.

"Sit back, shorten your reins and pick up your hands, then close your legs."

Nothing.

"Buck, since you're closest to her, will you demonstrate?"

Buck duplicated her position, then corrected it.

"This is how we do it at Deacons Hall," Amy protested.

"This is rebellion," Cap said.

"Over picking up the reins?" I watched them go around. "Walk please."

I had to think for a moment. "Let's do a bending line gymnastic."

Cap nodded and went to move standards.

***

"I'm not sure why Ami wants riding lessons."

Lockie shrugged. "I've been around a lot of kids and there are a million small reasons but there are only three big ones. Their parents want them to ride or they think it's a cool thing to do."

"What's the third?" I asked.

"You can't keep them off a horse."

"That was you."

"Absolutely."

The singing of the tree toads came in through the open bedroom windows. The night air was cool and rain was in the forecast.

"Why did I want to ride?" I wondered aloud.

"Escape," he replied.

"Why did I keep riding?"

"Because it was the only way for you to connect to another living thing."

"Why do I ride now?"

"Because you're so damn good at it and it's become part of who you are."

I snuggled up closer to him and fell asleep.

∽ 16 ∾

WE SPENT THE DAY bathing and braiding horses, Lockie supervising final rides while Greer was on the phone confirming arrangements and appearances. At the house, Jules was in the process of making the last of her Ambassador of Good Cheer gourmet lollipops depicting Oliver's face. Day, Cap and I were standing on buckets making rows of perfectly tight braids.

Cam and Freddi had left the previous day with the Acadiana horses to attend a very large, and prestigious show, the other side of the Hudson River. There were classes for him all three days, but the big stakes classes were on Sunday.

197

It was unfortunate Cam wouldn't be able to attend Miry Brook as I knew he would enjoy seeing Greer in her vintage style habit. Greer would have liked Cam to be at the show because no matter how heated their exchanges were, she found some comfort in the fact he hadn't turned away from her yet.

Dinner was served outside, with expertly grilled chicken and beef, light salads and finished with white strawberry ice cream. My grandparents told stories about their trips to ancient historic sites and all the food they couldn't eat. In the final analysis, it always came down to food for the Swopes.

Well after dinner was over and all the tales told, we helped clean up, then called it a night. Somehow, it was far less objectionable to have Buck staying in my room, than it had been to know Fifi was in my bed.

***

We were like a caravan arriving at the Miry Brook Hunt Club. In the lead was Lockie driving CB, Henry, and Tea in the van, followed by Greer driving Lockie's trailer with Spare and Wing, then Aly with Tango and Beau, and bringing up the rear was Day and Moonie.

A spot in the field, close to the building, had been reserved for us so Greer wouldn't have to struggle to get around. A golf cart for her use had been left nearby. The ladies from Aside Not Astride were next to us and soon had erected a small tent, with a table to offer information on side-saddle riding.

The grounds were wonderfully colorful and soon there was no room left to park, so many trailers had arrived. Another area was opened and Ellen Berlin hurried around, beaming with delight.

Nearing eight o'clock, my father arrived with my grandparents and Jules who efficiently began setting up a table to feed all of us for the rest of the day. My grandmother helped, and had donned a Bittersweet Farm baseball cap. If showing had been like this in the past, I probably would have enjoyed it a lot more.

"What do you need to do?" Lockie asked, coming up with a program in his hand.

"Gincy and Poppy should get on and walk the ponies around."

"Why don't we send Buck out with them? When is their first class?"

"Equitation on the flat. Should be around nine-thirty."

"Is the new girl supposed to show up today?"

"Ami? No, they're going to a dinner theater with a group of friends. She wouldn't have time, she said."

"Committed and interested, good combination," Lockie replied. "I'll get Buck on, you get the girls, and that will be handled."

I nodded.

Greer drove up on the cart. I could tell she was going to be putting many miles on that.

"The show photographer will be here in twenty minutes. Get everyone ready to have pictures taken. Day come up to the club house when you're finished. Ellen has questions about your painting and the auction. Have someone get Tea ready for me. I'll be back."

Before I could answer, she was driving away.

"I've seen drop fences that weren't as scary," Lockie admitted.

"She can become very focused."

"Just as long as she doesn't start breathing fire. We need to get these horses going. When are you going to get on CB?"

"After the Zuckerlumpen's equitation class."

Lockie looked at the program. "Leaving you one class between that and your hunter modern era class."

"That's what I mean, plenty of time."

"Get on and show him the grounds. I'm getting on Henry and we'll go together."

I looked into the van. "He's busy eating hay right now."

"Is this how you used to be at shows?"

"No, I was usually hiding from Greer and her friends."

"Come with me because I want the company."

I rolled my eyes.

"What if I need your company?"

"That's so unfair," I replied.

"So that's a yes."

"Yes." I went up the ramp to get CB and apologized to him as I took him away from his hay.

Day was getting on Moonie to prepare for her Pre-Green Hunter class. Cap helped me tack CB and I mounted. Lockie was already on Henry, and after leaving Cap with instructions, we walked down the drive to the ring.

On the far side of the building, the vendors had already set up their wares in the tents provided by the hunt club. Ellen Berlin wanted unity of design, which meant all the same. There were strict rules about flags flapping in the wind, music, or loud noises, any of which might frighten the horses. Most professionals would come equipped with earplugs, but amateurs, especially young riders, might not be aware of the help that could be.

"It's larger than I imagined," Lockie said.

"More people?"

"Yes."

"Greer and Ellen have worked hard to achieve this. The board of directors must be very pleased. The money, and publicity could give the club a welcome boost."

"Everyone has to work harder in a crowded field," Lockie commented. "The hunt club isn't exempt."

CB looked at a golf cart traveling past him but didn't seem bothered by it. "Do we need to work harder?"

"Equestrian sport is a crowded field overall but we do something different. We train slower and more thoroughly. We don't have to rent a property or pay off a mortgage as some professionals must do so time isn't bearing down on us at the expense of the horses."

We reached the warm-up area.

"Do these look like the first act of a wild west show to you?"

"No. When I was about eleven, I saw one of those once at the Earl Warren Fairgrounds. There were mules pulling a chuck wagon and someone riding a camel. A little girl galloped in front of me upside down in the saddle. Eventing was tame after that. So is any warm-up area."

My phone rang and I answered it.

"The photographer's here," Cap said. "Greer wants to know where you are."

"I'll be there in a few. Bye."

"We have to get back to the van. The photographer wants us."

"I'll skip the portrait. I'd rather have a shot of Henry this afternoon. You go ahead and I'll have a look at the outside course."

"Okay. Will you be back for the ponies?"

"Wouldn't miss pony equitation on the flat for anything." Lockie smiled.

"Equitation was good to you," I replied, taking the back way to the trailers where the photographer was already shooting Poppy and Gincy, grinning and looking adorable in their bows and braids.

I dismounted and asked for a conformation photo of CB, which the photographer was glad to do. We moved across the drive and found a spot with trees as a background. He did his best to look regal for the first few shots, then started playing around, asking for a cookie and letting his ears turn to listen to all the activity. Since it wasn't important and the ponies had their class in a few minutes, I thanked her and let her move on to a more serious horse, Moonie. Then I gave CB cookies and he was very pleased with me.

Between Cap, Aly Beck and the Hambletts, we got the ponies warmed up and to the in-gate before the announcer called the class.

"Go out there, have fun. Don't worry about the other riders. Find a place on the rail and stay there. They'll avoid you. You're going to sit up straight?"

"Yes, Talia," Poppy replied.

"And?"

They thought for a moment.

"Smile," Gincy said.

I patted their knees. "That's right. Tango and Beau love you now, and no matter what happens out there, they will still love you."

The gate opened and they entered the ring.

Lockie leaned over to me. "No one ever gave me that kind of pep talk before I entered the ring."

"What did your trainer say to you?"

"Usually something like 'Okay, you little nitwit, see if you can stay on and not embarrass me.'"

I turned to him in shock.

"We've all had them. At one show, the owner heard him talking like that to me, and the following day, the horse and I were moved to another barn. That's when my career really took off." Lockie touched my hand. "No, I won't tell you his name so you can email him and give him a lecture. It wouldn't do any good. Some people you can't reach."

"Lockie."

"It's true, Tal. Watch your *Zuckerwuerfel*."

The ringmaster asked for the class to trot, and soon, not immediately, all the riders had gotten their mounts to trot and had found the correct diagonal. It reminded me of my own equitation classes and I remembered, while no longer being judged on the exact position of my foot in the iron, in about an hour, I would be in the same ring, trotting around on the rail, too.

The riders reversed and trotted in the other direction. They walked, then cantered. Poppy and Tango were blocked by a slower pony who kept breaking into a trot and a horse to her inside so she couldn't move out of the way. Gincy had the rail to herself and was intent on riding what appeared to be a dressage test, it was so serenely executed.

The class changed direction and cantered again. This time, Poppy made sure she was in the clear.

"She thinks," Lockie commented. "That's good."

"Poppy is very easy to work with. Would you like to take her on?"

"No, she adores you. Gincy I would like to see ride in with Buck once in a while."

"They're not on the same level at all."

"No, but she can do dressage with him. He's not far beyond his cowboy days."

The ringmaster asked them to walk and line up in front of the judge. One girl couldn't stop her pony and the ringmaster had to go to the track to slow her down.

"That girl will fall off in the over fences class," Lockie commented.

"What do you think will happen?"

"He'll run out at a fence, but she'll keep going in the direction they were headed in. Splat. Then he'll run around the ring and five people will be out there trying to catch him. He'll probably step on the reins and break them, if not the whole bridle. She'll cry."

"Her mother will cry," I added.

"That, too."

The ringmaster walked back to the center of the ring with the ribbons.

A girl on a small hunter was pinned first, and she had been on point throughout the class.

When Gincy was pinned second, we all cheered and applauded wildly. Lockie whistled.

Poppy was fourth and I assumed it was because of the problems being boxed in. The point of showing was to get the judge to see you when everything is going right. Unfortunately, the judge must have seen her when everything was going wrong.

We congratulated both of them, they were both happy with their ponies, and we all went back to the van.

Cap had CB ready for me when I arrived, Lockie gave me a leg up and we returned to the warm-up area full of horses, most Thoroughbred, some indeterminate.

"Have you ever shown in the green hunter division before?"

"No, just junior," I replied.

"There's nothing I can tell you about it. He's going do the course and the judge will decide if she likes that much expression. Thirty or forty years ago, his style was in fashion."

"Now, not so much."

Lockie nodded. "Do some *voltes* at the trot, half pass. Canter. He should feel light in your hands."

I nodded and trotted away.

CB was sharper than at home, and there was so much to look at, his attention was drawn rapidly from one thing to another. As soon as I shortened the reins, he focused on me. We warmed up, did a few serpentines as best as we could snaking through the crowd, then moved on to the half pass, finishing up with an extended trot then returned to Lockie.

"What a show off," Lockie said, giving CB a big pat on the neck. "The minute you started, everyone around me began staring and pointing."

I shrugged.

"Good for you!"

The class was called, and we went to the in-gate. Everyone from the farm was there to encourage us, which made accounting well of ourselves more important than usual.

We entered the ring for the green hunter under saddle with the rest of the assorted horses and I took a deep breath. Piece o' cake, I thought. That's what I really needed, a piece of Jules' cake instead of being at a horse show. I blocked out all the other horses, riders, flags, announcements and equitation class being run in the ring nearby and focused on the ride.

CB trotted smartly around the ring. Too smartly. He was supposed to be turning the tips of his toes green by brushing them through the grass, and instead, there was a moment of suspension in each stride. As soon as we reached the bottom of the ring, he really had to show off and do his swish. Fortunately, it wasn't dressage where we would be alone, so I guessed the judge wouldn't care very much if she even noticed because there were so many other horses in the ring.

We cantered, then reversed direction and repeated the drill. The ringmaster asked us to walk and then line up.

Good. It was almost over. I could almost feel CB's interest in the process waning as he flicked his tail back and forth with increasing force.

A lithe Thoroughbred who didn't bend his knees placed first. Pinned second, I took the ribbon instead of having it slipped onto CB's bridle and we exited the ring to cheers from Team Bittersweet.

I slid off and received big hugs from my grandparents then father, then Jules. Everyone told me how perfect CB was, and how the other horse didn't deserve the blue, even though he did. Then we headed back because the Zuckerlumpens had a fence class coming up.

Lockie fell into step next to me. "You're in the process of breaking your jinx."

I laughed. "I couldn't pin over Nicole and Greer. We were always in the same classes."

"Do you know how long I would have let that stand?"

"Thank you."

"That doesn't make up for what happened to you."

"Yes, it does." I bumped his hip with mine.

Chapter 17

We had a wonderful lunch with all our friends dropping by to share with us and leave with cupcakes or Oliver lollipops.

It was not Poppy's day to win, nor Gincy's either, as there were experienced pony riders competing against them. They understood and enjoyed the show anyway, looking forward to their one retro pony over the outside course class.

Lockie and I had taken them out into the broad expanse of field and walked the course. Some of the young riders, and older ones, were concerned about the solid fences over real terrain, but to the Zuckerlumpens it was all elements they had seen before.

I felt as though I was doing my job and was pleased.

We stopped by the club house where Greer was giving a talk on side-saddle history while wearing her beautiful habit. She had the crowd mesmerized.

"She's the best thing I ever did," Victoria said, coming up alongside me.

"I agree."

"Did she ride this morning?"

"No, she's just doing the side-saddle and that's this afternoon. You're doing the retro class?"

Victoria glanced down at her pegged canary breeches. "I thought it would be fun and good research."

"Excuse me?"

"My next book might be set in the first half of the twentieth century. For some, there were very fine years," she said.

"The 1920s."

"Yes. Everyone had money or the reasonable expectation they would be able to get it. Then in 1929, it all fell apart. That's emotionally interesting, don't you think?"

"I think I'd rather hear about the good times than the bad," I replied.

Victoria squeezed my arm. "Of course, you would. You're your mother's daughter. Good luck in your class." She walked away.

I stayed to listen to Greer's talk, which was met with enthusiastic applause. After answering some questions, we walked back to the van together.

"You'll get the green hunter reserve championship," she said. "You should feel good about that."

We had pinned second in the over fences class because CB was being quite expressive and the Thoroughbred was not. He was exactly the ideal show ring hunter, so it was expected they would do well.

"Yes, but I'm really looking forward to seeing you in the side-saddle classes."

There was one on the flat and one over the outside course.

"What did my mother want?"

"To wish us well."

"What does she really want?"

"She said she was researching a new book set in the 1920s perhaps."

"Did Pete Bouley come to support his son?" Greer asked.

"I don't know but it looks like the Coopers did."

I could see Kate and Kerwin sitting in the shade and Fitch was standing talking to my father and grandfather. Everyone seemed to be having a good time.

"This is the best show I've ever attended," I said to Greer.

Betsey Harrowgate was mounted and heading for the ring as we arrived. "We have trouble. Nova and her coven have arrived. They're just milling around by the club house now but they're not here for that. I'm going up there to find out what's going on."

"Don't kick a hornet's nest," I said.

"She's the one who's doing the kicking," Betsey replied and trotted off.

"Oh boy. There is security here, isn't there?"

Greer nodded. "I'd better alert Ellen."

Jules came up to me. "What's wrong?"

"I don't know that there is, but there might be. Some women here who want to ban all male things."

"Did I hear that right?"

"Yes. Side-saddle is a symbol of female oppression. Their way to spend a fun afternoon is to protest such injustices and raise awareness of how horrible men are."

There was a short pause. "This seems like a Fifi thing," Jules replied.

"It does, doesn't it? Greer's explaining this to the show committee. I'm sure it'll amount to nothing," I said and went to help Greer get ready for her first class.

By the time we reached the ring, the protest had begun.

"Throw off your shackles, remove your chains," they repeated softly to us as we passed.

"Not freaking again." Cap scowled.

"Ignore them," Greer advised from atop Tea. "They're just attention-seekers. Don't feed the trolls."

We continued to the ring where the side-saddle riders were already entering for the flat class.

"Have fun," I said to Greer, giving her apron a final straightening then she joined the other and the gate closed.

Jules came up next to me and gave me a squeeze. "I'm so proud of you both."

I smiled. "Thank you."

Team Bittersweet was there to cheer Greer on as she rode as well, it seemed to me, as the women with years more experience. They all looked wonderful wearing habits with nipped in waists and long flowing skirts. The show photographer was busily engaged in getting action shots of the class and a crowd had formed to watch because few people had ever seen side-saddle in real life before.

A woman from New Jersey won the class with Betsey pinning second, and Greer coming in third. We cheered as the rosette was slipped onto Tea's bridle. As she left the ring, Greer looked more pleased than I ever remembered.

She was deluged with compliments, which she accepted but insisted we not spend a moment more on her. The ponies had their retro class to do.

Of course, Greer was right. We had to rush to get the Zuckerlumpens changed, on the ponies and to the outside course in time. They rode it just as though it was Lockie's course in the field. Poppy attacked it, while Gincy's approach was to calmly take each of the natural fences as if they were no big deal. The girls looked adorable in the old clothes Aly had found for them, even if the jodphurs were a little big on both of them.

"Definitely sugar lumps," Lockie said to me. "No wonder you love working with them."

"They're so forgiving of my mistakes."

"You haven't made any mistakes with them. Your instincts are spot on."

"Maybe."

"Yes. Now go change into your old clothes and get CB ready. They'll be calling your class and you'll be out here acting like you have no responsibilities."

"Such as?"

"Winning the green hunter division so the farm gets publicity."

"The Thoroughbred has twenty points toward the championship and we have twelve. Do the math."

"I don't have to. Anything can happen. Go."

Buck had changed and was preparing Wingspread for his round on the outside course. He had done well in the morning classes but, as with the ponies, there were many riders his age who possessed more sophistication in riding hunters. Buck considered himself an event rider, and had ignored the dressage phase. He was good and stuck to the saddle but he wasn't refined yet.

Lockie would get him there if Buck was around long enough. I didn't know what the future or even the summer held for him since Mr. Bouley seemed so unconcerned with parenting his son.

I crouched down to my bag to fish out the pegged breeches.

"Hey."

Standing quickly, I turned to see Cam.

"What are you doing here? I thought you had a stakes class this afternoon."

"The show was cancelled. There was a complete power outage in town. With no electricity, there was no water for the horses or humans. Everyone started to pack up and go home so Teche and I decided to see how you were doing."

"I'm glad you did. Your parents are...I don't know where everyone is. Buck's here. Cap's riding Spare in a jumper class. Lockie's watching her. I'm getting ready for my class."

"What's with the protest? Ban all what?"

"Oh. Ban all the male things. It's a protest against side-saddle."

214

Cam couldn't have been more confused by this. "What?"

"I would suggest you go have them explain it to you but you're a male and should be banned."

"I don't need to know. Where's Greer?"

"Her outside course class is going soon. I was just going to change and take a walk."

"So, change."

I grabbed the breeches, went into Lockie's trailer and swapped my good stretch breeches with the soft leather at the knee, for ridiculous cotton twill pantaloons that billowed around me. The leather patches were as stiff as cardboard. I could only hope that in the short while it took to ride the course, I wouldn't keep thinking how extraordinarily uncomfortable the retro breeches were.

We met Team Bittersweet in the spectators' area just as Tea and Greer began their ride. My grandmother was so excited, and in disbelief that it was possible to jump sitting aside.

Jules grabbed for my hand as Greer headed to the first fence, a gate. "You two are making me crazier than Fifi ever did."

"She'll be fine," I said.

And Greer was. She rode the course as though side-saddle was a very familiar style and not something she had learned in the past months.

For a moment, everything behind us fell away and it was like being transported into an earlier era. There was nothing of the modern world in front of us. It was better than a movie or a ride at Disney World. This could be real.

It was real. Watching, I understood why riding side-saddle could be so appealing. It was not just a new skill, it was a passage to a different world.

As Greer and Tea took the last fence, I glanced over to Cam. He couldn't have been more focused.

In that moment, I was certain. "You love her, don't you?"

He didn't take his eyes away from Greer. "That's not the kind of thing I'd admit if I did, is it?"

"Don't give up on her."

The round ended to cheers and applause, and we made our way to the exit to greet her. My father helped her dismount and gave her a hug as Buck led Tea away from the crowd.

"Don't do that again," my grandmother said. "It looked very dangerous."

"It's perfectly safe," Greer insisted. "I'll meet you back at the encampment, I need to check on the blacksmithing demonstration. He was having trouble with his coal fire."

"I'll go with you," I replied, and gave Cam a look to encourage him to join us.

Cap, Cam and Lockie walked with us to the main building but before we got there, Nova and her friends were blocking the way. The group had grown in size and there were now about twenty-five women wearing tee-shirts and face paint.

When I looked closely at Nova, I could see she was wearing fresh tampons as earrings. That coupled with the #BanAllTheMaleThings tee-shirt was a hint that this was the wrong direction to go in.

"I think we can leave this until later," I said, grabbing Lockie's arm.

"What?"

Lockie wasn't paying attention and I didn't want him to.

"Oppressor!" Nova shouted at Cam.

Greer transformed into major royalty. "Do your dignity a favor and leave now before you're escorted off the property."

"This is a public event. We have the right to gather and protest!" one of the women shouted back.

"It's private property. Public property is owned by the state. Tch. And you went to college. Didn't do much for you, did it?" Greer asked.

Lockie began laughing. "I like those earrings. If you need them later in the day, you can just—"

I grabbed him and pulled him back a step but Cam saw the tampons dangling from their ears and began laughing twice as hard as Lockie.

"Ban All The Male Things!" the group shouted.

"Ban all uninvited guests," Cap called back.

"Throw off your shackles, remove your chains!"

"Get lost!" Cap replied.

"Remove the chains men have put on you!"

"Why don't you find a real cause to support? Animal welfare," I suggested.

A crowd was gathering around us as the shouting continued.

"Women should be free!" Nova screamed, dropped her sign, and pulled off her shirt.

Lockie and Cam began laughing harder. A second later the crowd began laughing and pointing.

Mothers were dragging their daughters away and covering their eyes. Fathers and boys were enjoying the performance art.

"Learning to spell would be good," Greer said evenly.

Nova looked down. Across her chest she had meant to paint the words "All men are beasts". Instead, she had added an "r" in the most unfortunate spot.

The security guard arrived as the coven began removing their tee-shirts. "What's this? No, this is not permitted!"

"You can't tell us what to do!" One of the protesters shouted. "We won't follow your male laws!"

A town police officer walked up to her, looked down at the billboard on Nova's chest, and nodded. "Tell it to the judge," she said, escorting Nova and the group off the hunt club grounds.

Cam put his arm around Greer. "Gracie. There's never a dull moment with you."

18

"THAT'S A BAD THING," she said.

"No. That's a great way to live," he replied.

I watched them for a moment, then realized this was the time to leave them alone. "Lockie, I've got the class, so help me get CB ready."

"I'll get Henry ready for you, Lockie," Cap said as she jogged past us.

Ten minutes later, we were out in a field warming up. CB had settled down since morning, and wasn't as distracted by each horse that went past.

I pulled up next to Lockie.

"I'm useless as a coach to you," he said.

"Why would you say that?"

"What can I tell you about riding CB here?"

"I want to refute that statement but..."

"There's nothing to say. Go out and ride the course. Try to maintain an even pace. Most horses will pick up speed as they go along."

"Butch didn't," I replied as we walked to the entrance.

"Why am I not surprised to hear that?"

"Butch was good for me."

"I would never suggest he wasn't."

We stood as the Thoroughbred who had won both classes that morning started the course. Both the horse and rider seemed tentative as they approached the first fence.

I could understand why. It was a straight vertical gate and gave the impression of being solid. There were breakaway pins but it was the real thing otherwise.

The horse got over it and cantered for the next fence.

"She needs to pick up her pace for this course. That's a show ring hunter pace."

They made it over the second fence because the horse was a good athlete and they proceeded to the real stone wall.

This was not a problematic jump for me because we had a stone wall in the lower field that everyone jumped all the time.

The Thoroughbred said no thanks and without any persuasion from the rider, he ran out. She kept going in the direction they had been traveling and landed hard on the turf, while he cantered away.

My number was called.

"Good. I can finally give you some coaching. Don't do that."

"Okay." I smiled and trotted onto the course we had walked earlier.

"Piece o' cake, CB," I said, asking for a canter.

Turning for the first fence, we were hand galloping, and flew easily over every jump. When I asked him to slow to a trot, he continued to canter as I made a large circle. I think he wanted to go again.

Team Bittersweet was there with cheers and praise I didn't deserve. It had been CB doing all the heavy lifting.

A few minutes later, our number was announced over the loudspeaker and we went out onto the field.

"Winner of the Green Hunter Championship number 73 Talia Margolin riding um...Fr...Froodigin G...Gist, something."

"Freudigen Geist!" Team Bittersweet called out together.

The crowd laughed.

A huge rosette was pinned to his bridle and a large silver bowl was handed to me. We stood, relatively quietly, for the photographer, and then left the field.

Greer removed the rosette so it wouldn't annoy CB and Cap took the trophy as we all headed back to the encampment.

"Told you," Lockie said. "You broke the jinx. Happy?"

"Lockie."

I held my hand out to him.

"Tal..."

"I don't care."

"People will talk."

"I still don't care."

He reached up and closed his hand around mine.

 The End

Visit us at the Bittersweet Farm Facebook page for all the latest information,

Sign up for our mailing list and be among the first to know when the next Bittersweet Farm book is released. Send your email address to: barbaramorgenroth@gmail.com

Note: All email addresses are strictly confidential and used only to notify of new releases.

About the Author

Barbara got her first horse, Country Squire, when she was eleven years old and considers herself lucky to have spent at least as much time on him as she did in the dirt. Over the years, she showed in equitation classes, hunter classes, went on hunter paces, taught horseback riding at her stable and went fox hunting on an Appaloosa who would jump anything. With her Dutch Warmblood, Barbara began eventing and again found herself on a horse with great patience and who definitely taught her everything important she knows about horses. She now lives with Zig Zag, a Thoroughbred-Oldenburg mare.

Printed in Great Britain
by Amazon